Thine Eyes
of Mercy

Jamie Lyn,
King Jarrok is,
waiting for you!
Chaos be with
you!

DANIELLE M. ORSINO

Danielle M. O

Thine Eyes of Mercy

Birth of the Fae Book 2

—

4 Horsemen
Publications, Inc.

4 Horsemen
Publications, Inc.

4 Horsemen Publications, Inc.
1497 Main St. Suite 169
Dunedin, FL 34698
4horsemenpublications.com
info@4horsemenpublications.com

Cover designer by Jen Kotick
Typesetting by MC
Editor S. L. Vargas

"Dragor" Dragon concept by: Danielle M. Orsino
Dragor Flying by: PandiiVan
Map is illustrated by Daniel Hasenbos–he goes by Daniels Maps
Makeup Artist Denise Apostle, IG: @DeeMakeupnhair_hair
Cover photographer Julia Juliati

Library of Congress Control Number: 2021948857

Print ISBN: 978-1-64450-407-9
Audio ISBN: 978-1-64450-405-5
Ebook ISBN: 978-1-64450-406-2

Table of Contents

"You know how the humans will view a small-winged creature such as yourself. They are religious fanatics.""
~ *King Jarvok.*

DEDICATION

Compassion is something we can never have too much of. We need it for ourselves, each other, animals, and the planet. Compassion is the trait of the strong, for to have compassion is to know our own weaknesses and be willing to understand everyone has flaws and to choose empathy instead.

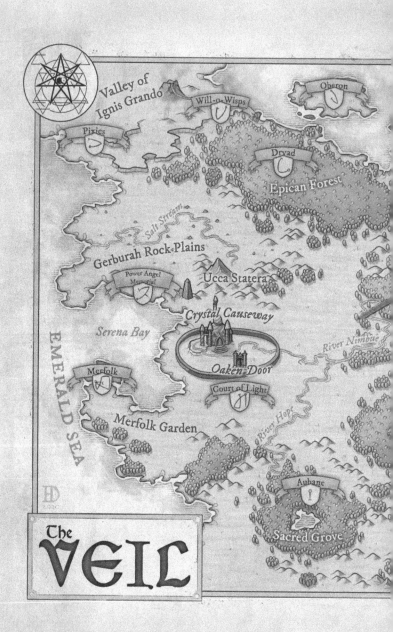

The VEIL

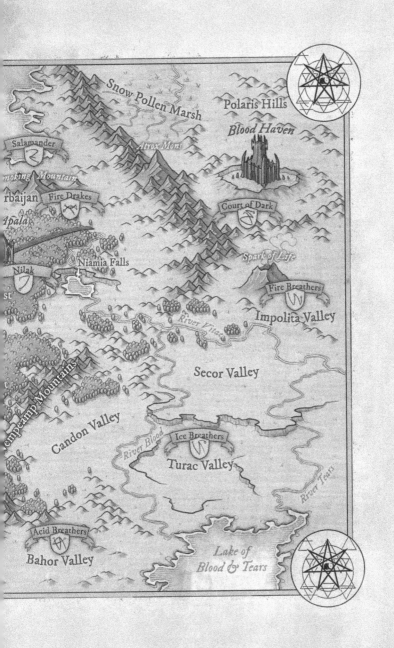

Snow Pollen Marsh

Polaris Hills

Blood Haven

Salamander

Atrox Mons

moking Mountain

rbaijan

Fire Drakes

Court of Dark

pala

Spark of Life

Nilak

Niamia Falls

Fire Breathers

st

Impolita Valley

River Vinac

Secor Valley

empeamp Mountains

Candon Valley

Ice Breathers

River Blood

Turac Valley

River Tears

Acid Breathers

Bahor Valley

Lake of
Blood & Tears

Acknowledgments

My brother Billy: For his bravery, service to this country, and allowing me to use his time in the Army as inspiration.

PMD.

My pups Carlos and Penelope: I never thought two little fur balls would steal my heart and become such sources of love.

Jacob: Chaos be with us and thank you.

CBS: Thank you for being my Yoda on another journey into the Veil.

The 4Horsmen I hope you enjoyed another trip into the Veil. I look forward to more.

Pandii: One of the most amazing artists this side of the Veil.

Karen Kay: My Fae Godmother.

Morris Freeman: You are part of the Fae now. Chaos be with you!

Wendoura: The Fae have gained a star.

To my Fae friends and the Bookstagrammers: This book is happening because of all of you. Thank you for taking a chance on a new author. I appreciate each one of you! Thank you and Chaos be with you!

PROLOGUE

66 **I** have begun watching the Fae. Yes, I do adore the fact these former angels have changed their names—more than I can possibly tell you—simply because it pisses off the Creator. Ha! When you call yourself *'The Creator,'* you might have an overinflated sense of self-importance.

I digress: I find the Fae more interesting than the Creator's super ego...

Queen Aurora of the Court of Light Fae and King Jarvok of the Court of Dark Fae are exhausted and battle-worn after centuries of fighting. Which I find quite amusing! The Little Queen put up a cute fight against the King. I have seen him in action. He is formidable. Good for her.

The humans have worshiped both of the Fae courts since primitive times. Kudos to the Fae for figuring out the inherent power of human worship. Of course, I am doing it so much better. The Fae were the centerpieces of the humans' polytheistic pantheon of gods and goddesses for millennia until the Dark Fae no longer desired to share with their counterparts. That was quite shrewd of the Dark Fae King. The humans' adulation enhances the Fae's existence, allowing their Magick to grow exponentially. King Jarvok, insisting there were not enough human worshippers for both courts, declared war. Jarvok believed his victory was assured. A dire miscalculation—the Court of Light refused to go quietly.

As Queen Aurora and King Jarvok descended further into the toils of combat, their human worshippers suffered. The two became obsessed with defeating each other, neglecting their cults, groups, and temples in favor of games of war. Fae factions lost their worshippers and, therefore, their source of power until whole factions perished. The perfect situation for me to slide in and begin establishing my own religion.

With factions lost to Oblivion, it became obvious to both courts that they could not sustain their conflict. Level heads prevailed, but it took great loss and almost a millennia of battle before both sides concluded a meeting should take place to discuss a treaty. Each court drew up their conditions, planning to assemble on neutral territory and exchange demands in hopes of ending the bloodshed.

Now, I sit and observe. Let's see how long their little experiment lasts."

Chapter One:
A Truce of Sorts

D ragor grunted and snaked his neck toward the land below, jerking his head upward as he caught a scent. His sickle tail snapped, causing an echo to disturb the solitude.

Sitting astride his back, King Jarvok patted the dragon's side. "You are correct, my friend. It is time to go. Today, I will end this." Jarvok shook his glistening white hair back and slipped on his Black Kyanite helmet. The stalagmite points cast a long, distorted shadow, mimicking a crown of thorns. *Will I be the savior of my kin or their doom?*

Jarvok had mounted Dragor, chief of the Draconian Faction and his personal dragon, well before dawn to journey to the fringes of the Court of Dark's territory. Now the pair stood atop Atrox Mons, the highest peak of the black mountain range bordering his fortress of Blood Haven. Literally translated, Atrox Mons meant "terrible mountain," and it was: jagged rock protruded from its midnight façade, and no light penetrated where it loomed over the land. Dragor's claws dug into the calcite and granite rock, dislodging boulders that disappeared in long, silent drops.

Jarvok ran his hand over his face, cupping his jaw. The war between the Court of Dark and Light had lasted close to a millennium. What should have been a quick clash had turned into a long, drawn-out game of bloody tag. Each Court gained an inch only to lose miles and lives, the monotony of it playing repeatedly like song stuck in your head. Out of the gory clashes, the Blaze Battalion, Acid Assault, and Ice Invaders was born. However, even the elite Draconian fighting troupes with their raw power could not deliver that final kill shot to end the Court of Light.

Jarvok gazed out at the morning fog settling into the lower valley. He inhaled, holding it for a second, his eyes closed and his mouth turned up as he relished the cool, crisp mountain air. Then he exhaled and let his eyes float open. Jarvok took in the full view from Atrox Mons. Everything fell into place here—his thoughts congealed, his dreams solidified, and his Chakras balanced. The mountain was majestic, immovable, feared and respected. It was everything Jarvok had hoped to be as a leader to his kin.

Dragor snorted and jumped off the mountain, diving downward. His amber eyes were rimmed in pale blue rings and covered in a thin, translucent membrane to protect them. The wind pinned back his royal purple–tipped head feathers—he looked like an arrow as he gained speed. Then, his large wings unfolded, a tinge of purple reflecting in the sunlight upon the outer edges. The dragon banked effortlessly through the clouds, touching down in front of the Dark Fae troops.

Jarvok's thoughts flowed back to the war and how they had arrived at this day. He had never expected Aurora to have the stamina or fortitude to keep fighting, but more than that, she was formidable. She had surrounded herself with the right Fae to guide her. He was confident he would have defeated her in the end, but the longer they were distracted, the more human worshippers they would lose to the newer religions.

First, it was Judaism. Their mystical branch of Kabbalah allowed for some of the pagan practices to remain, but it tended to skew more toward the Court of Light. Hinduism was helpful due to the number of gods and goddesses, but still, it was not enough. The Christianity movement did not help either court; it had caught on far too fast, speaking out against paganism and encouraging its followers to wipe out those who practiced the old ways. The main concern with Christianity was that Jarvok's Creator, his Creator's "son," and even Lucifer were the central stars. Jarvok wondered if it gave, Lucifer and his demons more power as well. The idea of Lucifer and his horde having more control on Earth worried Jarvok; he needed to keep his kin safe, and ending the war and re-establishing his power base were paramount. The Dark Fae had neglected their humans during the war. *Destroying the Court of Light cannot take precedence over the good of my kin,* he thought. He needed human worshippers to keep a strong power base, and the more this single-God religion spread, the less power he had.

A small unit of his Weeper army followed in formation behind him. Jarvok's most trusted lieutenants marched between the king and the Weepers. He was due to sign the truce, but should something go wrong, he wanted to be prepared. The Dark Fae king held up his right arm to halt their movement while he surveyed the area. His musings had taken up much of his time, and the group had arrived sooner than expected at the first checkpoint.

Zion, Jarvok's second-in-command, caught up with him to see what the next move would be. "My liege? What troubles you?"

Jarvok scoffed. "Nothing, Zion, but I don't trust anyone, least of all Aurora. I want you to take the Weepers and submerge them under the bridge. If Aurora keeps her word, there is nothing to be concerned about. If not, then on my signal, kill them all." He dismissed Zion, watching him gather the Weepers.

"Asa!" Jarvok commanded. The Fae with blue-streaked hair rode forward on a burgundy ice-breathing dragon. The dragon had cobalt tribal swirls on each side of the cerulean triangular scales running down her back, denoting her young age. As the dragon matured, her plumage would fill in and her swirls would be covered. The dragon's name was Yanka. She was smaller than Dragor but strode up to the much larger creature Jarvok rode, head held high, keeping up step for step.

"Yes, my liege." Asa punctuated her greeting with a quick bow of her head. Like her dragon, she was petite, but her fierceness was palpable. The Black Kyanite armor was a stark contrast against her luminescent skin. Peeking out from her mask was one pure white eye with no iris or pupil. The armored mask was contoured around her face, covering more now than when the war had first begun. Jarvok wondered if Asa's scars had gotten worse since the war started, but today was not the time for such questions. The swoops and curves came up to the top of her head, ending in what looked like a halo of stalagmites. Her crystal-blue left eye set off her matching sky-blue hair, which danced with streaks of light. She was striking. Everything about Asa was in juxtaposition. Asa was hard and soft, light and dark, but her unique ability made her even more of a walking contradiction.

"Asa, I have sent Zion under the bridge in case Aurora gets any ideas. You will be my second for the rest of the mission. Tell me what you see."

Asa blinked. Her white eye gave off a bright, incandescent glow. Her voice vibrated with power, echoing as if she spoke from within a deep chasm. "Aurora ... near the bridge with five of the Illuminasqua following close behind. They make no effort to conceal themselves. The Aubane Faction leader is with her as well. There are no war color banners flying. She comes in peace, my liege."

King Jarvok leaned in. "Is Desdemona present?"

Asa furrowed her brow, eyes closed and head tilted. "Yes, my liege. Desdemona rides next to Aurora at her right, leading her Illuminasqua." She shook her head.

"Thank you, Asa. If Desdemona is there, Aurora may be expecting a fight. We must be on our guard."

The king ran his middle finger under his helmet, feeling for the sunken valley. The scar on his right cheek ran from his ear to the corner of his bottom lip. He vowed to pay Desdemona back for her gift. There weren't many who could challenge him, but Desdemona had and survived it. He respected and hated her, but the ratio was not equal.

Desdemona was not just any Virtue; she was the only Power Angel ever exalted to that status, on the recommendation of none other than Jarvok's former commander, Archangel Gabriel. Commander Gabriel had assembled a troop of Powers from different brigades to scout for rogue Angels planning to defect to Lucifer. Unbeknownst to Gabriel, he was actually the one being set up. Lucifer ambushed the small group. The demons descended upon Gabriel's Powers so quickly, half of the scouting troop was slaughtered in a few breaths. Lucifer squared off against Gabriel—brother versus brother—but it was common knowledge Lucifer was the stronger one. There was a reason he was the one who could stand against their Father. Soon, Lucifer had Gabriel pinned up against a tree by his throat and stood ready to send his brother to his Oblivion.

Desdemona intervened. Posing as a defector, she took Lucifer by surprise, driving her Elestial Blade into his shoulder, severing his arm. Desdemona took her body weight and cut straight through the tendons and muscles. His arm hung limp, barely attached but for a few stray pieces of ligaments. Her blade had cauterized the wound. Lucifer didn't care; his rage was all consuming. The almighty Light Bringer was down to one arm, but that did not mean he was defenseless. Gabriel had enough time to crawl away and call Archangel Michael, Desdemona's commander, for help. However, Gabriel's exit meant leaving Desdemona to take on Lucifer's wrath alone. How she survived Lucifer, the Light-Bringer's, full rage and physical assault remained a mystery. Speculation suggested Lucifer's grievous injuries had prevented him from unleashing his full power.

When Gabriel returned with Michael, it took the Archangels' combined strength to drive Lucifer back to Hell to nurse his wounds. They found Desdemona beaten and bloody, barely alive. For her sacrifice, Desdemona was exalted to the status of Virtue. She was allowed to keep her Elestial Blade. Desdemona was sent to Earth as the sentinel of the Virtues. Jarvok reckoned her name choice, Desdemona, came from her confrontation with Lucifer.

She was a true warrior at heart and Aurora's personal bodyguard.

Jarvok respected the bodyguard's cunning nature and appreciated that Desdemona, not Aurora, was behind the Illuminasqua, the Court of Light's elite force. They had a terrifying reputation, second only to his Weepers. The brilliant design of their ranks was undeniable; no one knew exactly how many Illuminasqua there were because they were indistinguishable. The members were female Fae with a strong, athletic physique. Each associate had one dark braid, resembling the sea at midnight, and black diamond markings under each eye, matching their lips, which complemented pale-grey eyes. Their uniforms were black, including their hoods, button-up vests, pants, and thigh-high boots. They wore gold shoulder pauldrons with the septagram, weaponized wrist gauntlets, and a choker with each elemental symbol in gold. They carried double-serrated hooked swords, known as the Harbingers. The swords were sheathed into their boots because the blades were a last resort. The warriors were skilled in hand-to-hand combat, including a special martial art known as Syncron which gave them basic control over the elements.

The only difference between the Illuminasqua is their tattoos. Each time an Illuminasqua made a kill with her Harbinger sword, the weapon transferred the victim's essence into a tattoo on the Illuminasqua's body. The tattoo which would be the victim's name in a sigil could materialize anywhere on the warrior.

Desdemona was the only Illuminasqua who allowed herself to be seen up close; under any other circumstance, to see an Illuminasqua meant imminent death. Jarvok took pleasure in knowing the humans and Fae feared his Weepers more than Aurora's Illuminasqua. For all intents and purposes, the female Fae warriors stayed within the walls of the Court of Light protecting their queen or carried out stealth missions of assassination. The Illuminasqua were the Court of Light's last line of defense.

Jarvok's Weepers incited terror, but that was not his initial intention. The Dark Fae king wanted his army respected for their prowess and military astuteness, not dreaded for ruthlessness and savagery. Jarvok had set out to save the abandoned Powers. Unfortunately, many of them could not acclimate to life outside the command. These Powers had been in the Brigade for so long that when Jarvok gave them their identities back, they had refused. Many did not remember their individual nature before the Brigade. They required the regimented lifestyle the Power Brigade provided, with its hive mentality and coping mechanisms. Without these, they had time to think about what had transpired, including their abandonment by their commanding Archangel and the Creator.

Many soldiers chose Oblivion over the burden of having free will for the first time in millennia. Jarvok had no choice; forcing them to be individuals was not working, even though he had thought it best. While he realized he was forcing conformity, as had his Creator, Jarvok was ill-equipped to help them cope with the ravages of war without reverting to the old ways, which he interpreted as a form of slavery. He swore it was a step backward. Jarvok wanted these Powers to have a say in their lives. He branded their armor with their names but did not push to use them.

Jarvok had set up training exercises to keep the soldiers busy, placing Zion and Asa in command. This had helped, but some soldiers still compulsively picked at their Angelite disc scar, causing it to reopen and bleed. The blood running down their foreheads and past their eyes gave the illusion of crying, earning them the nickname Weepers.

The harder they trained, the more disconnected the soldiers became. They continued to mutilate themselves to feel something, anything, and now their wounds were a source of constant bleeding. The war between the two courts had kept his Weepers occupied, but with the call for a truce, he worried for them—idle hands and all.

On the other hand, the Weepers' taste for human blood had grown since the war, starting something Jarvok had never imagined. Or perhaps he had ignored the signs; the war had started so long ago, he was not sure. They were harder to control. He also worried about their growing fury toward humanity. The Weepers were the most efficient killers on the planet—no one could deny it—but like any caged animal, they wished to break free.

Some of Jarvok's Weepers had flourished with the war. They took orders and fell in step, but after each battle, Jarvok would receive reports of Weepers having episodes of uncontrollable rage. Asa would use her empathic abilities to bring them back into the fold. Then, it began happening far too often, and her efforts were less successful, fewer returning from their fits. The king was always the one to deal with those Weepers; he never asked anyone else to carry out his orders. He was their king; therefore, they were his responsibility. Their blood would stain his hands and his alone.

Jarvok recognized deep down that he was one of them. In a way the Dark Fae all were Weepers, as every Weeper was once a Power Brigade Angel. The difference between them now? His Weepers no longer had the sense to select what to kill and what to leave alone, and he did. Their trauma from the many wars and the abandonment had left them incapable of higher-level functioning. He thought the war with the Light Fae would give them purpose, but it had only inflamed their brutality. Jarvok had hoped their rage toward their Creator could be harnessed to focus on the Virtues, but instead they were finding it much more fun to take out the humans. Each mission ended with higher human casualties. It wasn't all from the Weepers, but it was enough to prompt him to agree to this meeting with Aurora.

This brought him back to his original ethical conundrum. He could not in good conscience keep the war going? But if it would protect the majority of his kin should he? But what about the emotionally damaged soldiers? While he felt for these Fae, he would not shed more unnecessary blood. This was why he had decided to put his sword down and end the fighting. Today, Jarvok, king of the Court of Dark, would speak with Aurora, queen of the Court of Light, and come to a mutual understanding benefiting his kin, *all* of his kin—the good, the bad, and the damaged—because they were all his. No Fae would be left behind, not while he was king.

Jarvok and his army stopped at the Bridge of Oroki. Two square black obsidian and blue kyanite pillars greeted them. Sigils of warning were carved into the megaliths, stating that this was "The Court of Dark's territory— beware: all who cross will meet Oblivion."

It was the only way to cross over the clear blue Nimbue River and the Forehelina Forest marking the division between the Courts of Light and Dark. At the halfway point on the bridge was the Archway of Apala, neutral territory for the courts. Jarvok and Aurora had agreed to meet there.

The long curves of Forehelina trees with their sinuous branches and lavender foliage hung over the riverbank, creating a curtain of serenity. Jarvok steadied Dragor, patting the large beast on the neck, soothing his sudden agitation. A true Fire-Breather, Dragor hated walking over water. He preferred to soar above it. "Easy, my friend," Jarvok said. "I am sorry, but we must walk the bridge. I promise if all goes well, we can fly home when we are done."

Dragor snorted in reluctance, placing one large claw on the curved wooden surface. The bridge moaned under his weight, but he pressed onward toward the Archway of Apala.

Sunlight broke through the clouds and seemed to chase them away, rays of light bouncing off her armor in staggered moments. Wearing battle armor never felt natural to Aurora, and yet for far too long, it had been her uniform. She shifted, uncomfortable under the weight of her shell. The gold armor felt heavier today, perhaps because it was the last day she would don it. Her golden headband matched the sweeping designs of her breastplate and shoulder pauldrons. The armor cast a long, proud shadow as she floated above the puffs of pink grass leading to the Bridge of Oroki.

Theadova trotted along next to her; Aurora no longer rode the white stag. As he was the leader of the Aubane Faction, she felt it was disrespectful, for half his faction had met their Oblivion during the war. Others of her party did continue to ride at the Aubane's insistence, however. It helped the faction feel useful to their queen.

"Your Grace, I would have been happy to carry you," Theadova said, glancing back at his kin as the rest of the entourage rode the other oversize white deer. A fleeting look of sadness passed over his dark eyes, his lips moving but no words escaping them. It seemed he was counting their numbers.

Aurora observed her friend and confidante. Yes, she recalled riding on his back before this war and how he saved her that fateful day when they met the humans for the first time. But today was about endings and new beginnings. "I know Theadova. But you are a leader and I want the Dark Fae to see you as such."

"King Jarvok will be riding Dragor," Theadova retorted.

"Would you argue with a Fire-Breather?" Aurora answered.

Theadova nodded. "Point taken, Your Grace."

"Theadova, were you counting your numbers before?" she asked.

The white stag dropped his head. "Yes, our mating season was not what I expected. Our females are having issues carrying to term."

Aurora placed her hand on his side as they walked. "Have you spoken to Lady Sekhmet?" I believe once we sign the treaty and we can concentrate on our humans, this will resolve."

Theadova exhaled. "Yes. Lady Sekhmet is helping us, and I trust you, my queen." He ended the conversation, and Aurora allowed him, not wanting to press the stag.

Desdemona rode at her queen's right, ever vigilant. The captain's grey eyes scanned the landscape, her muscles coiled in a state of warrior-like readiness. Desdemona's right hand sat steady on her hip, free to use her Elestial Blade if needed, and her left hand rested gently around another member of the Aubane faction's gilded antler. The three bishops followed behind.

Aurora was sure it did not matter to Desdemona that they were meeting Jarvok to sign a peace treaty. The dedicated captain would not let her guard down in a situation where the Dark Fae king was involved.

"My queen?" Desdemona's voice rose an octave as they came upon the entrance to the Bridge of Oroki.

"Yes, Desdemona?" Aurora was fully aware her captain looked forward to talking about strategy.

"I scouted out the Archway of Apala a few days ago. I attempted to bring this up to you yesterday, but you were preparing the treaty. The bridge itself is a narrow passage without coverage. Once we are at the site, the circular platform of the archway leaves us open for strikes from both above and below. Should Jarvok decide to attack, I'm afraid my options will be very limited."

Aurora appreciated Desdemona's pragmatism. "Captain Desdemona, this is a peace treaty negotiation. There is no coverage for a reason: it is neutral ground. I must have a certain amount of trust in King Jarvok."

Desdemona's mouth pinched upon hearing her queen speak Jarvok's name in such a manner. "Forgive me, Your Grace, but trust and Jarvok are not synonymous, believe me. He has certainly made contingency plans." She narrowed her gaze, her expression flat. Aurora took note.

"I'm sure he has, but those are his ways—not mine. I'm going for peace with no intention to fight. There has been enough bloodshed."

Desdemona bowed her head, and when she lifted it, her features were blank. Aurora hated when she did that. After centuries of friendship, Aurora knew it meant Desdemona was not happy with whatever answer she had been given. The queen put her hand over her stomach as it tightened into a knot.

Desdemona and Jarvok had a long history. Mutual dislike was one aspect, but there was a dose of respect for each other's strategic mindset. At times, it could border on paranoia. Aurora knew Desdemona would not let this go so easily. But the queen believed this war needed to end today. Too many lives had been lost—too many friends gone.

My ego let this war go on for far too long.

Aurora believed she could best Jarvok, but she was not a warrior queen. She was a nurturer—it was in her blood. By ending this, Aurora could provide a supportive environment for her kin and protection the only way she knew how: through diplomacy and wisdom. She raised her arm to halt her traveling companions. The Bridge of Oroki stood before them.

The spiraling quartz pillars were speckled with sunlight, their points topped with large golden seven-pointed stars, denoting the beginning of the Court of Light's territory on this side of the bridge.

"Take a moment," Aurora said. "We will not be able to rest once we begin crossing the bridge, so center yourselves. We cannot afford any emotional outbursts." Aurora studied her followers. "You all must recognize what we are here for. Peace. Do not allow yourselves to be goaded into an exchange with them. I am counting on all of you, my friends, as is the Court of Light. Bishop Geddes, please prepare for the treaty reading and brief the others on what will transpire at the archway."

Geddes acquiesced.

Her followers watched their queen walk away, their idle chitchat creating enough white noise for Aurora to lose herself in the hushed currents of the Nimbue River.

One of Aurora's followers sat at the bank of the river with her white deer. Her skin, the color of the finest bronze sand, luminescent like all of the Fae, was awe-inspiring. Her midnight-black hair was streaked with pale pink and mint green, resembling the colors of a lotus blossom. The Fae's doe-like eyes were copper-hued, flecked with rose gold. She was tall and thin like a willow tree branch but still maintained a feminine physique. She did not control elements like the other Fae. Sybella was an Oracle. One was born in every generation after the Oracle before had expired. Reva was her predecessor.

Aurora recalled the day Sybella was born, Lady Ambia running into the contemplation room to inform the queen a new oracle had come to them. "She is here and this one is strong my queen," the healer said.

Aurora looked down at the fluorite floor and saw there were not shadows indicating they were in the midst of the eclipse.

"Tell me Lady Ambia, what makes her different?" Lady Ambia had an apprentice present the baby to her queen, swaddled in silk of pink and green, was the infant and still with the mother's placenta over her eyes.

"Lady Ambia, what is the meaning of this?" Aurora exclaimed.

Lady Ambia took her fingers and gently split the thin blue tinged membrane, placing the gore in into a hammered gold bowl. The infant's eyes remained closed for a few heartbeats, then she blinked them open, revealing her rose and copper eyes to the world. "She will have the gift of sight, my queen, as will her negative. I shall ring the bells and tell of her birth."

Now Aurora gazed upon Sybella, looking into those eyes and hoping her gifts would guide her through a challenging time. The gift of foresight varied in strength. Not every Oracle was able to fully explore this tool; they needed control and discipline. Sybella possessed the ability to center herself and tap into this energy. It was limited but still powerful. Sybella had described her clairvoyance to Aurora using the imagery of a sailboat on the ocean: she could predict where the sailboat would end up based upon the ocean's currents, but a change in the wind could blow the sailboat off course to parts unknown. The variables involved were exponential, and while the Oracles predicted the most probable outcome based upon the strongest energy current, they never spoke of an event as if it took away one's own free will.

Aurora wondered if Sybella's counterpart for the Dark Fae—Lady Zarya—was doing the same for Jarvok.

Aurora watched Sybella stroking her white fawn named Star due to the deer's icy, incandescent star-shaped birthmark on her flank. Sybella tilted her head, sensing the queen's approach. As she stroked the white deer, Aurora noticed a flickering of light occurring above the creature's head. Each time the Oracle touched the creature, mint green translucent antlers wavered in and out of focus. Star did not seem bothered by the play of lights.

"Lady Sybella, what is happening to Star?" Aurora asked, pointing above the deer's head. The Oracle paused mid-stroke, her hand delicately relaxed upon her deer's back. She gave a soft smile at her deer, then toward her queen.

Aurora's eyes widened as she clasped her hands against her chest.

"Is Star your familiar?"

Sybella shook her head and traced Star's celestial-shaped birthmark with her finger.

"No, my queen. A familiar has never chosen a Fae Oracle, to my knowledge. But that would be an event! Star is my kindred. We are bonded much like you are with your element. Her energy antlers you are seeing—" Sybella stroked Star slowly, and the pastel green antlers revealed themselves. Small sparks of energy danced from the edges like fireflies in a summer's eve meadow. "These represent the energy of our bond. The Aubane faction is more prone to bond to Fae. Perhaps it is why you feel such a kinship with Theadova."

Aurora tilted her head back, processing the information. "Theadova does have a calming effect. What else does your bond afford you?"

The Oracle rubbed her cheek against Star's. "Because she is my kindred, I can transfer her essence into other animal forms, so she will always be with me."

Aurora looked up at the canopy of lilac trees, a break of sunshine warming her face; its rays glinted off the intricate design of her circlet She closed her eyes and exhaled. Her shoulders relaxed, the heavy pauldrons seeming to want to slip off. Yes, the weight of being queen through a war was weighing on Aurora. "I like the idea of being able to take someone you love with you. It's a lovely sentiment and an amazing gift." Aurora opened her turquoise eyes, glittering with unshed tears. She blinked them back, refusing to release them.

As the queen turned her gaze toward the River Nimbue, there was no need for mind reading. Lady Sybella was well aware of the Fae her queen was wishing for in the blue water, the rainbow tail Aurora was hoping would not show itself. Besides, there were more pressing issues at hand than playing with memories and dancing with remorse.

"You did not wander over to ask about Star. You are wondering if this is the best way to end the war." The Oracle's voice was smooth with a lyrical lilt.

Aurora shook her head and painted a smile on. "You know me too well, my friend. I want to make sure I am doing what is correct for all of us."

Sybella continued to stroke and sing to her white deer, gathering her thoughts. "Jarvok is not a power-hungry ruler. He believes he was helping his kin, and though his methods were not ones we agreed with, he didn't start this war for selfish reasons. Jarvok has deep-seated issues, but he is not self-serving. You cannot defeat him on the battlefield, Queen Aurora." Her eyes met Aurora's, the rose-gold flecks flashing in the sun's broken rays. "If this war continues, we will all cease to exist, both the Court of Light and the Court of Dark. He needs this truce as much as we do." Sybella stopped stroking Star and held Aurora's gaze.

Aurora sighed. "This insight would have been nice to have two hundred fifty years ago."

At her mumbling, Sybella gripped her fawn's fur and arched an eyebrow at her queen. "My queen, I cannot speak of who King Jarvok was then, nor will I make such an attempt. It would be pure conjecture, not my gift. I can only speak of what may happen now if you both continue down this path. I have explained how my gift operates; it is for the benefit of all, not for the good of one." The Oracle gave a long, controlled exhale, her mint-green silk cloak stirred by a breeze. "If five Fae will fall from a steep mountain ledge, and I foresee their end, am I to tell them? Even if one of them meets their Oblivion by nefarious ways?"

Aurora shook her head, Sybella exasperation ghosting across her face. But she said nothing to the lithe creature.

Sybella continued with her lesson; either she did not care about her queen's annoyance, or she did not notice. She had advice she felt her queen needed to hear. "And what if I told you that because of my not saying a word, the faction would construct a stone wall, saving five hundred Fae lives over the course of time? If I had interfered, the wall would not have been built. As for the one Fae who died under suspicious circumstances, her offspring would grow up to become part of the Illuminasqua because she was imbued with a sense of justice and a profound respect for life, and she is now one of your captain's most trusted warriors. Ripples in a pond, my queen. Free will is sacred. Don't assume you should have had any information you were not given." Sybella did not wait for her queen to answer. She returned to stroking Star and singing.

Aurora gazed out at the aquamarine water of the Nimbue River as the willow branches skimmed the surface, their edges caught in its currents, fighting the pull.

The queen related to that. She stared at the river and the bridge, knowing who waited for her.

Aurora looked back at her kin, Sybella reflecting on everything the Oracle had enlightened her about. Sybella had not been her Oracle at the start of the war. Sybella was more powerful than Reva, and yet she had been her Oracle for only one year. Aurora faced her followers, taking in each one and lingering on them. She saw friends who had become hardened warriors. They had lost a bit of their heart, and that was too much. She also saw those who trusted her and hoped for an end to this, and today she would deliver on her promises. "Mount up!" she commanded her followers. "We march onward to meet the Court of Dark. This war ends now!"

The queen sounded more optimistic. Sybella smiled.

The Archway of Apala was the widest point on the narrow crossing, the crystal archway of raw aquamarine making a large circular platform at its highest point to accommodate a group of ten Fae for each court. The structure originated from deep below the river and came up through the bridge. The entire piece looked organic, as if the forest and the bridge were secondary to the archway. The cloudy light-blue crystal contained striations of white and hues of blue and green running throughout the magnificent pillars. The megalithic construct stood thirty feet tall with three sweeping archways. The keystone piece was a lone faceted translucent crystal stone in the largest arch. Sigils of the courts' factions were engraved on their respective sides. When the sun hit the center stone, its rays bathed both sides in spectacular, brilliant blue light, indicating neutral territory. Aquamarine promoted clarity, balance, and communication—helpful during negotiations. The crystal was an obvious choice for the building of the archway. Inside the middle arch, a reminder was inscribed that this was neutral territory, and it was taken seriously: "No blood shall be spilled in hate. Your word is your bond, as the universe moves through you. Break this oath and pay with your light."

King Jarvok waited at the archway, Dragor steady and watchful under him. Asa flashed her eyes. "They are approaching, my liege." Yanka shook her head and bucked, her tail swaying, the bridge complaining under the dragon's sudden movements. The Ice-Breather's cartilage tusks dilated and constricted, forming cold vapor puffs. Dragor stepped in front of the younger dragon; as her chief, his duty was to calm her.

Aurora's power wafted through the air well before she was seen. Any skin not covered by Kyanite armor had goosebumps from her power.

Jarvok snorted at her power push. "Amateur," he mumbled under his breath with an accompanying juvenile eye roll. A figure appeared, making no sound as it glided over the wooden slats of the bridge. Not wanting to admit it, Jarvok had to concede Aurora had a commanding presence as she floated. "It serves her," he commented to Dragor. "You look pretty commanding when you fly too." The dragon snapped his sickle tail in agreement,

There was a wobble as the bridge accepted new guests, and another figure appeared, the dark hair and marked skin a remarkable contrast to her queen. It was more than the regalia of the Illuminasqua uniform. Even the distance could not dull the energy crackling and searching him out. Jarvok recognized Desdemona. In her innermost part, she was still a Power Angel. Her energy signature called to him; it was familiar, like home. *Troll's balls.*

Jarvok dismounted and strode to meet them, Asa in tow. The two monarchs stood on their respective sides, bathed in the blue-green light of the keystone. Each met the other's gaze.

Neither spoke for several moments. Aurora sighed at Jarvok's stubbornness. "King Jarvok," she said because she knew if she waited for him, they would be here all day.

Jarvok held her stare. "Queen Aurora." His tone was flat.

Asa was the next to acknowledge the queen with the customary Light Fae bow of respect, learned from Prophecy readings at the Archway: her right hand in a fist over her heart. "Your Grace."

Queen Aurora was under no obligation to return the gesture, but in the interest of peace, she signaled to his third lieutenant with a simple, "Lieutenant Asa."

Jarvok glared at Desdemona, waiting for her show of respect.

Desdemona bit the inside of her cheek and followed Asa's lead with the same Fae greeting, followed by a terse, "Your Grace."

Jarvok gave a wry smile and touched his right index finger and middle finger to his forehead, breaking with tradition and offering her the customary Power Brigade greeting. He offered no words of greeting as was Power Angel protocol.

Desdemona scowled and gave Aurora a sideways glance.

Bishop Geddes waited for his cue to commence the ceremony, but with the tension between the two courts, he could not figure out when to call the peace treaty to order. He had fallen into the background for much of the time, too scared to draw attention to himself or the other bishops. Ward and Caer stayed so far back they were practically hiding behind the Illuminasqua.

Dragor decided now was a good time to let out a snort in their direction and watch the two bishops tremble.

Asa hit the Fire-Breather in his side. "Don't scare the bishops. It's too easy." She gave a little sneer. Aurora rubbed her temples, tiring of their cockfighting. She let out a long, slow exhale. "King Jarvok, are you ready to begin, or are we waiting on your tardy second-in-command, Lieutenant Zion?"

Before Jarvok could speak, Desdemona interjected, "My queen, Zion is already here."

Aurora turned to Desdemona, brows raised.

"Isn't he, King Jarvok?" A smug smile crossed Desdemona's painted black lips.

King Jarvok's jaw clenched before he returned to his stoic façade.

"Good. I was hoping you wouldn't disappoint me." The Dark Fae king glowered back at her."

Lieutenant Zion is underneath us," Desdemona said. "With about twenty Weepers, their iron-dipped spears pointed up at us." She paused. "I am sure they have been given orders to impale us on Asa's telepathic signal. So, there is no need to delay the peace negotiation waiting for Zion. Correct, King Jarvok?" Desdemona stepped forward, hands on her hips, head cocked to the side. The members of the Court of Light began mumbling.

"Can you believe he did that?"

"How did she figure it out?"

Caer and Ward were already wrangling their deer, ready to leave.

Aurora appeared unconcerned with the revelation, or perhaps, she was trying to convey nonchalance. She was not pleased with Desdemona's diplomacy skills, but she was more upset with her own naïveté. *Damn it to Lucifer, I should have listened to Desdemona on our way here. She said Jarvok would do something. Stay calm, Aurora.*

Aurora was not going to question King Jarvok; if it was true, it would be disrespectful to Desdemona. But Aurora was unable to read the king's expression, not with his helmet shadowing his face. She looked to her Oracle who gave the slightest nod, urging her onward.

"This is not how one begins a peace treaty, King Jarvok," Aurora said. "In the interest of full disclosure, I suggest you ask Zion and the Weepers to show themselves, or there is nothing for us to discuss." She remembered what Sybella had said: "He needs this war to end as much as we do." Aurora had to play this perfectly.

King Jarvok never took his eyes off Aurora as he spoke. "Lieutenant Asa, tell Zion and the Weepers to surface. They are dismissed." His voice was steady and sure. Jarvok made a curtsy-like gesture, as if asking Aurora if this would suffice.

Splashing resounded from beneath the bridge as the Weepers emerged from the river, marching in seamless formation, their poisonous iron-tipped spears in hand. Zion yelled an incomprehensible order, one the Light Fae did not understand, and the Weepers veered off toward the riverbank. Zion jumped up into the trees, the branches bending one after another as he climbed toward the sky. The air swirled with the lavender flowers shaken loose from Zion's climb, bringing the fragrance of lilac and musk.

A large winged shadow flew overhead as Zion reappeared at the top of a tree. His arms extended, he fell backward from the uppermost branches. Raycor, his white dragon with a full black tail, caught him and barrel-rolled, streaking upward. With a roar, she banked sharply left. Zion vaulted off her back and landed on the bridge like a dying leaf in the autumn winds, graceful and quiet. The Dark Fae settled in a crouch next to his king. Then he stood, his wet Kyanite armor glistening in the sunlight. He removed his helmet, revealing blue-black hair, the streaks of blue visible against the black of his Kyanite armor. His facial features seemed carved by an artist: large, almond-shaped dark-blue eyes, high cheekbones, and full lips set against marble skin.

Zion brushed his long hair back, revealing the telltale scar marring his almost perfect skin. In the middle of his forehead was a jagged three-inch, oval-shaped wound. He had been an original member of the Power Brigade and had taken out his own Angelite disc. The scar was deep and would never fully heal; any other Dark Fae born on Earth scarred their forehead with the Dark Fae's symbol out of respect. However, their scars were done during infancy by their healers and were more of a brand than the scars Zion, Asa, Jarvok, and others had endured.

Zion stood in front of his king. "You summoned me, my liege?"

"Show-off." Desdemona coughed, but Aurora shot her a look before it could go any further.

King Jarvok returned his attention from watching Aurora to Zion. "Yes, Zion, it seems the queen was uncomfortable with my preparedness, and it has been requested that you remain by my side for the duration of the talks."

Zion cast Aurora a glance. "As you wish, my liege."

Jarvok's second-in-command sauntered toward Queen Aurora. "I am sorry if I offended your peace process, Your Grace. The contingency plan was my idea to keep my king safe. My apologies." He bowed, watching her through his eyelashes, a soft smile crossing his lips.

Desdemona rolled her eyes at Zion's feigned sincerity.

King Jarvok's attention returned to Aurora. "If this settles your anxiety, can we get on with it?" He tapped his foot, his Kyanite boot making a hollow sound against the slats of the bridge.

Bishop Geddes cleared his throat, sensing the increase in tension. "King Jarvok, you are present to act as the emissary for the Court of Dark Fae and all the factions therein. Correct?"

Jarvok exhaled in frustration at the formalities. "I am not an emissary. I AM THE COURT OF DARK!" His gaze pierced the bishop, who swallowed and turned away, then posed the same question to Queen Aurora.

Her answer was authoritative, but softer in tone. "Yes, Bishop Geddes."

Bishop Geddes twitched his nose and raised his staff. "Please, each of you place your right hand on the stone's archway columns on your respective sides."

Both did as instructed.

Bishop Geddes projected his voice so that all could hear: "As we bear witness under the Archway of Apala, Queen Aurora of the Court of Light and King Jarvok of the Court of Dark meet here on neutral ground. No blood can be shed as the two stand with their hands on these columns. All who have accompanied them must obey these laws. So mote it be." He looked at each camp.

"So mote it be," the Court of Light replied, followed by the Court of Dark.

Asa stepped forward to address Aurora. "Queen Aurora, please present your Oracle."

Aurora gestured to Desdemona, who disappeared among her traveling companions for a quick moment. She re-emerged, Sybella at her right side. The Oracle dropped her mint-green cloak, unveiling a corseted gown with a long silk train composed of layers of different hues of purple. Around her neck hung the most precious treasure of the Court of Light: a charoite crystal necklace, the stone of the sacred path. Charoite was a rare, lilac-colored crystal that swirled with energy of its own. Every Oracle before Sybella had worn it, and every one after her would don this necklace as well, indicating their choice to volunteer their gift as service to the Court of Light.

"I present the Lady Sybella, the Court of Light's Oracle from the House of Helena." Desdemona gave her a sign of respect and stepped back.

King Jarvok bowed deeply to indicate his genuine respect for the Oracle. "My lady," he said with sincerity.

"My liege," she responded in the Court of Dark's vernacular. She returned the bow.

King Jarvok nodded to his followers, who all bowed, including the three dragons.

Sybella returned the motion and faced Jarvok. "I'm most touched by your demonstration of respect, King Jarvok." Her copper eyes were full of earnestness.

Desdemona interrupted the moment in her usual gruff fashion. "King Jarvok, please present your Or—"

Zion was one step ahead of Desdemona. He came forward with a woman, copy of Sybella, but different. Places that were light on Sybella were dark on Zarya like the negative of a photograph. The Oracles themselves were identical opposites of each other, or "negatives," but with no genetic links to the other. An Oracle would develop a strong psychic link to their counterpart as they grew. In time, their bond would intertwine them physically too, and if one became sick or injured, the other would develop the same symptoms. This connection always led the Oracles to their Oblivion; one could not survive without the other.

Zarya was the same height and body type, but her skin was dusted in silver instead of bronze. Her pink hair was streaked with black and pale green, and her eyes were most unusual, copper with a silver iris. The Oracle's silver complexion melded into her silver silk V-necked gown with bell sleeves. On her left wrist was a gold gauntlet with the Dark Fae symbols carved around a large bevel set with blue fluorite crystal. Blue fluorite amplified healing attributes and helped focus brain activity. It aided the Oracles in their prophecies by enhancing their connection with the collective. The bracelet held the power of the Oracles before her and one day would hold hers for the next Dark Fae Oracle. "I present the Court of Dark's Oracle, Lady Zarya, from the House of Rose Paw." While the Court of Dark did not follow the same political nuances as the Court of Light, the Oracles were the exception. They each took on their house's title as a sign of respect to honor their birth parents.

Queen Aurora bowed to Zarya. "Thank you for attending, Lady Zarya." The Court of Light followed suit with bows of respect.

The Oracles played by a different set of rules than the rest of the Fae. They often chose to live in seclusion, acting as the keepers of Fae history and observers of time, just as they elected to lend their gifts to their monarchs. The Oracles did not have to help the queen or king, but with this power came a duty to their kin. They were not indentured. The Oracles were held in high respect.

"My pleasure, Your Grace. I am happy to see the war come to an end." Zarya smiled, her voice warm and caring.

The Oracles were invaluable for many reasons, including their unique ability to read a Fae's intention from the written word. On this day, they would surmise if Aurora and Jarvok had any intention of double-crossing each other, based upon the monarchs' handwriting. This was why contracts were sacred and always requested between the Fae; your word was your bond .

With the Oracles in their places, Bishop Geddes addressed the two sides. "Queen Aurora and King Jarvok, we stand here today to negotiate an end to the bloodshed of the war between the Fae courts. Please have your Oracles exchange your requests for peace now." He watched the two leaders with caution, his neck corded. Tension filled the space between them.

Aurora nodded to Sybella. From her sleeve the Oracle produced a rolled parchment wrapped with ribbon, a rose quartz crystal dangling from the end. An unbroken magenta wax seal bearing a septagram sealed the parchment.

Jarvok gestured to Zarya, and she pulled out a parchment matching Sybella's with the exception of a braided black leather cord and bloodstone crystal at the end. An unbroken marbled red-and-black wax seal of the Court of Dark's crescent moon assured the integrity of the parchment.

The two Oracles exchanged parchments, and on cue, they broke the wax seals. The stiff paper unfurled in tandem, giving off a distinct scent. The Court of Light's smelled like white sage, earthy; the Court of Dark's was reminiscent of burnt cedar mixed with maple wood. The Oracles gave a quick read of the requirements from each court, checking the parchment for any deception spells.

Jarvok focused on Aurora, observing every facial tic and muscle twitch for signs of unease as Zarya read the queen's demands. Aurora seemed cool and calm.

Sybella and Zarya exchanged a glance.

"The parchments are free of any spell-play. We will begin our in-depth analysis of the words." Lady Zarya clasped Sybella's hand as she spoke. The two oracles worked efficiently, like the two halves of a whole. They were comfortable with each other, but the interaction was not warm; it was proficient and mechanical.

Fae on both sides stepped back in respect, allowing the Oracles to accomplish what they were brought in to do. The two Fae ran their fingers over the words, and as the letters glowed, the Oracles' eyes lit up. Then the handwriting awoke, as if stretching after a long hibernation. One by one, the letters lifted off the papers like vines growing; symbols trailed up the Oracles' wrists and around their arms until each Oracle was covered in the words once inscribed on the parchments. As the words crossed through their eyes, the Fae witnessing it saw the words flipped upside down and backward, unable to read exactly which words were being processed by the oracles. The Oracles saw how the parchments came to be with each passing word: they witnessed Jarvok and Aurora each drawing up their individual requests, who was present, who advised them, and what was in their hearts at the time. The Oracles spoke to each other in a language comprehensible only to the two of them. When they finished conversing, the writing scattered from their bodies, returning to the parchment. The Oracles nodded and directed her attention to her respective ruler, requesting private counsel, well out of earshot.

Sybella addressed Aurora: "Your Grace, King Jarvok's intentions are clear and for the good of his kin. His main concern is for his Weeper army. He needs them to continue to have a purpose; making them the gods and goddesses of atonement gives them that. It is not for sadistic enjoyment against humans or a power play." Her verdict was resolute.

Aurora paced, biting her bottom lip, rolling her head from right to left in an attempt to release the tension in her neck. "Is that all you see, Sybella?"

"Jarvok is a very pragmatic ruler. You need to be strategic and cover all your bases. Jarvok will look for any reason to question you, my queen, but your requests were read with pure intentions; he has nothing to doubt you on. You included a system of checks and balances by ensuring the Court of Dark receives the same amount of worship during the winter solstice and autumnal equinox. You were fair and equitable in your requests. His past actions were fueled by a feeling of abandonment. I believe we can all empathize."

On the opposite side of the Aquamarine pillars, Lady Zarya glanced at Dragor, who spread one gigantic black iridescent wing as she approached King Jarvok. Zarya smiled at Dragor. His wing folded around them, providing them privacy. The bridge moaned in concert with the dragon's movement. "My liege, Queen Aurora's intentions are pure. They are fair for the Court of Dark. Her motivations are to keep her kin safe."

Jarvok scoffed.

Zarya cleared her throat, continuing with her analysis: "She will honor the treaty, but do not push her on the human agenda of reproduction."

His head snapped to look at her. "Why?" His tongue rolled in his mouth as he spoke, as though he were anticipating a taste of the sweetest nectar. He hoped Zarya was about to tell him a delicious secret about Aurora. He leaned forward, his lips curling upward in a predator's grin. Lady Zarya paid her king's dramatic response no mind. "The queen is still hurting from her friend Lady Serena's demise. Allowing endangered Fae to reproduce is a small way of dealing with her loss. Should you push her to leave this out of the treaty, she may do the same for your Weepers' stipulation, knowing what it means to you."

Jarvok bowed his head, bringing his right fist to his scar. It was not what he had wanted to hear. His Weepers clause was the lone piece binding him to this treaty. He began pulling at the nape of his neck, winding the hairs around his fingers as his jaw ticked. "Will she honor her word if I sign it as-is?" The air hung heavy with his inquiry.

"Yes, her written words match her intention, my liege," Zarya answered with unfaltering confidence.

Jarvok clucked his tongue against the roof of his mouth.

The two Oracles met under the archway, followed by their monarchs, who placed their right hands to the columns for a second time, signifying that they would agree to each other's terms.

Bishop Geddes took his place between the two rulers, his bellow disrupting the contemplative silence. "Oracles, have we come to a resolution?"

Sybella spoke first. "Yes, on behalf of the Court of Light. We agree to the terms set forth by the Court of Dark. I have deemed King Jarvok's words to be of pure intent for his kin. We accept."

Bishop Geddes turned to Zarya.

"Yes, on behalf of the Court of Dark. We agree to the terms set forth by the Court of Light. I have deemed Queen Aurora's words to be of pure intent for her kin. We accept."

The Oracles lifted the parchments up, Sybella with her right hand and Zarya with her left. A faint glow emitted from each of the Oracles as the parchments levitated, hovering one above the other, shimmering in the blue light of the archway. Then the Oracles joined hands, and the two parchments melded into one.

In a single voice, the Oracles spoke: "You are all witness to the creation of the Treaty of Bodhicitta, a wish for enlightenment so the Fae will never spill each other's blood again. The rules of the treaty are as follows:

The Court of Light will govern summer and spring. They are to be worshiped during these times by humans.

The Court of Dark will govern winter and fall. They are to be worshiped during these times by humans.

No Fae court can interfere with the politics of humans in a nefarious way. Both must work to preserve the Fae courts equally. The Court of Light may act as advisors to the royal families as they have done, but they must not influence the humans against the Court of Dark.

No Fae court will incite or influence human war.

Reproduction with humans is forbidden unless to preserve a dying Fae lineage. If the mating results in a child who has more Fae characteristics than human, the child must be raised in the Veil as a Fae. A changeling will be left in the child's place. The changeling will expire within a few days. The human donor will have the opportunity to mate again with a Fae for a child of their own if they so wish, or they will have one favor of a Fae line to be used upon their discretion, within reason.

The Court of Dark must not interfere with humans in a malignant way, but they may act as gods or goddesses of atonement for human wrongdoing; if provoked, the Court of Dark's Weeper army will dole out punishment.

No side shall spill the blood of another Fae without permission or provocation, or it will be seen as an act of war.

Zarya pulled a galena crystal blade from her pocket, holding it aloft for all to see.

The Oracles again spoke in one voice: "Should either court break any of the treaty's rules, intentionally or unintentionally, it will be seen as an act of war. Your word is your bond. Please seal the treaty."

Aurora bowed and accepted the blade, pricking her right index finger until a speck of blue blood was visible.

The treaty floated in front of her. She signed and spoke the words: "As it is above, so it is below. My blood is my oath; this I swear. So mote it be." Her signature sizzled on the treaty and glowed.

The Oracles announced, "What is written in blood cannot be undone. So mote it be."

Sybella wiped the blade clean with the hem of her dress and handed it to King Jarvok, repeating the stipulation. "Your word is your bond. Please seal the treaty."

The king bowed and declined the galena knife, using his own Elestial Blade to cut his index finger until blue blood ran down. He signed the treaty, uttering the same oath. "What is written in blood cannot be undone. So mote it be." His signature sizzled and glowed, invoking his promise.

The Oracles raised their eyes to the sky. "What is written in blood cannot be undone. So mote it be." They lifted their hands over their heads, and the treaty spun and wrapped itself up. "You have all borne witness to the signing of the Treaty of Bodhicitta by the Court of Light and the Court of Dark. Queen Aurora and King Jarvok, tell your kingdoms the war has ended. Go in peace." The Oracles released their hands, and the parchment disappeared.

Aurora removed her armor at the archway, arranging it in a neat pile.

"Queen Aurora, what is the meaning of this?" Jarvok pointed to the pile of armor, his brows coming together. Asa and Zion exchanged a puzzled glance. The shine of the metal reflected the incredulous stares of the queen's onlookers.

Aurora smiled at their confusion. "Simple, King Jarvok. Our war is over, and I intend for no Fae blood to ever be spilled again between us. Therefore, I no longer need battle armor against the Court of Dark. I will keep my word, and I have faith you will as well. I lay my armor down." She looked at him with trust and sincerity in her turquoise eyes. She wanted to see his eyes, though she was unable. His helmet cast a long shadow over his face, the stalagmite points creating a halo effect.

Jarvok mounted Dragor, shaking his head at her gesture. "It is a nice sentiment, Queen Aurora, but that is the problem with a bleeding heart: in the end it bleeds out." Dragor jumped from the bridge, catching an air current, his sickle tail splashing the blue water before he gained height. His black shadow broke the purple canopy, followed by Zion and Asa's dragons close behind.

Chapter Two:
"King Henry VIII I am, I am"

Queen Aurora readied herself, dressing in royal finery. During the waxing moon, she listened to requests from royal families via her bishops. If the royal family had been loyal to the Fae, they might be granted an audience with Aurora. It was a formal affair.

The bodice of her gown was azure-hued chiffon, pleated around her neck, exposing her shoulders. Gold bangle bracelets with inlaid raw crystals decorated her upper arms, the gathered silk chiffon of the gown creating a wing-like illusion. Precious gems such as diamonds and rubies held no value for the Fae. Quartz, lapis lazuli, and citrine were the gemstones of the world and the true magick of nature. The crystals held energy of time past, acting as the emotional graveyard of the Earth. The gown was open at her back, exposing her luminescent Fae skin, though it was not flawless like the rest of her kin's. Down the queen's spine were symbols representing each faction of Fae that had died in the war; she branded her body to remember their pain and to ensure they would never be forgotten.

In Aurora's eyes, she had failed as their queen. She should have protected them; therefore, she would wear their sigils on her body for all her days. On occasions like this, Aurora dusted the symbols in gold so that they stood out. She made sure her royal garb never covered them. Her capes were always sheer, silk chiffon, draped low upon her back. This cape was hand-dyed to resemble the pattern of light reflecting on water, and the material billowed behind her when she walked.

The skirt of her dress—ivory silk chiffon—skimmed her hips and fell sumptuously to the floor. Embroidery twirled around the hem of the pleated overlay with shades of blue silk chiffon in between; it looked like ocean waves peeking out from the bottom of her skirt when she walked. Gold metallic thread delicately displayed the same symbols of the fallen Fae lines as those on her back, including her precious Serena's Merfolk line. The dress's brilliant cyan hues were her homage to Serena. They reminded Aurora of how the ocean appeared when the sun shone on the water when she would wait at the shore for her friend—and how the ocean looked when Serena broke the waves, the light playing over the water and encircling Serena's rainbow tail. Aurora smiled. She adored the dress.

The final touch was the crown atop her cardinal-colored hair, which was gathered into a simple bun at the nape of her neck. The center of the crown highlighted the cracked Angelite disc gifted to her by Serena; the Mermaid had said it came from the mysterious Shooting Star, a Power Angel attempting to return to the Shining Kingdom's gates. Aurora felt she owed her reign to that

Power Angel. She carried their Angelite disc as tribute to their sacrifice. She often thought that if the Power Angel had survived their fall, the war between the two courts would never have happened. But she might never have been named queen by the rest of the Virtue Angels left to fend for themselves after their abandonment. She raised her palm to her head, closing her eyes and centering herself. She would not get lost in such musings.

Aurora fixed her crown and waited for her guards to open the doors. Each guard placed their right hand over their heart in tribute to their queen and opened the doors to the Great Hall. Queen Aurora took a breath as Lady Serena's sage words flowed through her mind: "Every gal should wear their invisible crown ... always, Rory, even you. Chin up, or else your crown slips." A smile graced her lips, and pulling her shoulders back, the queen of the Light Fae entered the Great Hall.

The Great Hall was as the name described. It was a formal room made of quartz crystal and was the highest point in the castle; as such, it received the most light. The floors were clear quartz with each Fae line's symbol placed as a tile leading to the throne. Each wall was created from the crystal representing the element of that direction. The south-facing wall of amber represented Fire. Air was represented by the east-facing wall of citrine, Water by the west-facing wall of aqua Aura crystal, and Earth by the north-facing wall of green tourmaline. In the center of the room, a large throne made of celestial quartz sat with a gigantic seven-pointed crystal star hanging above it. The star represented the four elements, the sun, the moon, and the spirit of the universe. When they came together, they represented the light within all living creatures.

The star was constructed of a rare crystal known as a Super Seven: amethyst, cacoxenite, clear quartz, goethite, rutile, smoky quartz, and lepidocrocite naturally formed into one. Known as the stone of higher consciousness, this amalgamation of crystals balanced and energized all seven Chakras. It was exceptionally rare, and therefore, the perfect physical representation for their star.

Queen Aurora invoked the Guardians of each wall, warding off any unwanted energies from her sacred space as she had done many times before. She raised her arms and spoke, her low voice imbued with a trace of huskiness and a hint of power: *"Guardians of the Watchtowers, I, Queen Aurora, summon thee, stir and call you to witness this rite and to guard this hall. Hail and welcome!"*

The Magick selected its four representatives of the High Court. Aurora never questioned how; she trusted the universe. Her hunch was it has something to do with the elemental connections and who the Magick felt pulled toward that day. Aurora did notice certain guardians repeated, like the Selkies seemed to be a favorite of the water element. She had counted in the last two months, and a Selkie had been called upon to act as a Guardian several times. Without a word from Aurora, a gale-force wind lifted the Guardian of the East and flew her to her position. She stood at the wall and announced herself: *"East bears Air: wind soars. I now stand where there was none before, Your Highness."*

A fire raged, and out of the flames another woman appeared at the south wall. *"South frees Fire: the flames roar. I heed your call and stand where there was none before, Your Highness."*

The earth rumbled, and a woman rose from the cracked crystal floor. She stood at the north wall as the ground sealed shut. *"North cradles the Earth: a seed grows. I bow to thee, Your Highness."*

To finish, a rainstorm concentrated at the west wall formed a puddle, and from the puddle a woman rose, guarding the wall. *"West springs Water as it flows. I bow to thee, Your Highness."*

Yes, the West guardian was a Selkie. Her aquamarine long hair and large, round eyes resembling the ocean at midnight were telltale Selkie traits.

Aurora placed her hand over her heart in acknowledgment of the Guardians' service. She turned to the room. *"All the elements become one; protect my kin and those who enter therein. Cleanse their hearts with Water; burn their hatred with Fire. Grow love within their hearts like a seed from the Earth and sweep away their pain with Air. Destroy those who enter without purest intentions. Blessed be."*

When bringing humans into her kingdom, Aurora was very cautious. Her weightless gaze scanned the Guardians before she took her place upon her throne. Aurora lifted her eyes to the geometric cutouts in the ceiling, aware her captain of the Royal Guard, Desdemona, had Illuminasqua hidden somewhere in the lotus flower carvings. Aurora knew Desdemona far too well; she was nothing if not conscientious. Desdemona had expressed to Aurora that when they received humans, the palace was open to invaders, regardless of the war being over. Aurora would bet her crown Desdemona paced the Crystal Causeways on the east side of the palace at this very moment. She almost wanted to send a wind gust just to prank her but decided against antagonizing the warrior Fae. She signaled to the guard to allow her first visitor in.

The hinges of the heavy doors creaked open, and Bishop Ward entered. He placed his right hand over his heart, giving tribute to each Guardian. Then he stood at the foot of Queen Aurora's throne. Fae did not kneel to their queen; Aurora felt it was too much like praying. Instead, they bowed with their right hand over their heart as a pledge of loyalty. Bishop Ward bowed, his golden hair tied in a low ponytail falling forward, while he waited for Queen Aurora to address him.

"Merry Meet. What tidings do you bring to me on this waxing moon?"

Bishop Ward lifted his head from his obeisance, his cape falling forward. The bishops wore a new uniform of white brocade to symbolize their importance to the queen. Their coats were embroidered with the symbols of the elements in white metallic threading. The buttons were made of sea glass, a remarkable contrast to the stark white of the uniform. Bishops also wore a horizontal bar over their hearts. Every gold bar represented two hundred years of service as a bishop. Gold was used because it took all four elements: Earth to find the raw material, Fire to melt it, Water to cool it, and Air to harden it. Bishop Ward had seven gold bars; he was close to receiving his eighth.

Each bishop wore a unique cape. Their capes were white and floor length, closed on their left shoulder with a special clasp: one side was a star, and the other held the symbol of their element. When the two sides of the clasp came together to close the cape, they finished the septagram. The undersides of the capes were lined in crimson silk, indicating their control over their emotions and their individual elemental power. Each bishop brought their element to their queen—Fire stokes her ideas, Earth grounds her, Water helps to let her ideas flow, and Wind carries her ideas to her kin. They held no loyalty to their respective factions, only to the Fae kin as a collective, to which they pledged their service. The bishops in power had always been Virtue Angels, but now there was Awynn, who was born of the Earth. The rules changed for these Earthborn Fae. Aurora had decided Earthborn Fae, choosing the life of bishophood, would begin training at age ten to gain the utmost control of their elemental gift and to learn the path.

Bishop Ward represented the Caelam Faction, connecting him to the element of Air. The back of his cape was embroidered with his faction's Air symbol. The final, and perhaps most prized possession of a bishop, was his elemental staff. Once a bishop was strong and disciplined enough to wield absolute power over his element, they would go deep into the Veil and meditate with the purest form of their element: Fire tested by flowing lava; Air tested by facing a tornado; Water tested at the seafloor; and Earth tested in the deepest cavern. It was not known what transpired, but if they survived the test, the staff and crystal would present themselves to the bishop. They returned with total control over the element, and the staff allowed them to amplify their power. Bishop Ward's staff was teak and cradled a piece of raw, deep blue tourmaline crystal at the top. With a single thought, Bishop Ward could call a hurricane or a tropical breeze.

Bishop Ward smiled, sweeping his cape behind him as he addressed his queen. "Merry Meet, Your Grace. I present to you his Royal Highness King Henry VIII of

England. He wishes an audience with Your Grace. Will you grant him this request?"

Queen Aurora rolled her eyes and leaned her temple against her fingertips. Her dealings with King Henry VIII had always been complicated. He changed his mind almost as much as he changed his queens and mistresses. "Does he bring tribute for my kin, Bishop Ward?"

King Henry was not loyal to any religion, regardless of his title as head of the Church of England. Queen Aurora was acquainted with the true politics behind his schism with the Pope and his marriage to the late Anne Boleyn. Gossip and religious rhetoric aside, Aurora had a point to make about the king's lack of respect when asking for help, especially when his requests were about only power or lust. Both of these she often refused. He would try charming her and end up leaving in a huff. She put up with him because he allowed her pagan followers to continue without bother.

Bishop Ward spoke up, breaking into her thoughts. "Yes, Your Grace. He brings the Fae sweet cakes and fine wine."

With Bishop Ward's announcement, horns sounded, and human dancers entered dressed in white chiffon. Minstrels followed, playing music. Four men carrying a lavish table decorated with gold and silver plates topped with frosted cakes paraded in after. Streamers and ribbons waved from the table in colorful rainbow tails. The human men and women undulated to the music.

Then the music abruptly stopped. The dancers knelt and the horns blasted again, announcing the arrival of King Henry VIII. A shadow appeared at the open doorway; he was tall but gone was the taut, athletic build of his youth.

His girth eclipsed the light from the windows behind him. King Henry posed in a red-and-gold embroidered velour jacket trimmed in fur. Underneath it was a white-and-gold embroidered shirt with ruby buttons. If there was a belt, it could not be seen under his rotund belly. He adorned himself with a fine gold-and-pearl trimmed jerkin, which glittered in the light. He wore gold rings on every finger and scratched his beard as if to show them off. The king paused for a moment, drinking in the attention.

Henry was pompous, and Queen Aurora abhorred his vainglory. She glared at Bishop Ward. He would have had to have brought the extra humans over through the Oaken door, so he was complicit in this circus. She rubbed her temples for a moment before sending a wind gust through the hall to blow out all the candles. The Guardians stiffened. She put her left hand up to steady them and relaxed her shoulders. "King Henry, what is the meaning of such fanfare?"

King Henry gave the queen a deep, gracious bow. "Forgive me, Queen Aurora. I was demonstrating my gratitude. I thought thy audience was deserving of a celebration. I meant no disrespect." His voice was thick with false English charm.

Oh yes, he is quite charming! His full lips under that beard and devilish green eyes could still charm many ladies, but I am not a lady. I am Fae. Aurora sat back on her throne. "Your tribute is adequate, but next time, skip the show. Oh, and Henry, one last reminder." Aurora leaned forward, resting her chin on her hands. "Do not even think of addressing me as an inferior."

The king bowed his head. "Certainly, Your Grace. I appreciate your haste in the way of our discussion."

However, Aurora wasn't done with the king. "I believe you forgot your manners, Your Highness. You are in my court; here, you kneel in front of me." She stared at his half bow.

King Henry glanced around him, hesitant to go along with her request, but finally, he acquiesced, bending one knee at a time. Aurora's face pinched at the crackling and popping of his knees as the joints curved in their great effort to reach the quartz floor.

"Many apologies, Your Highness. I was taken in by the moment," he said through gritted teeth.

"Now you know why I don't like all the trimmings. People tend to lose their heads." She smirked, hoping he would enjoy the reference.

The king cleared his throat and fixed his collar. "Yes, Your Grace." He flushed pink, embarrassed to be admonished.

Queen Aurora grinned and gestured for a sweet cake for herself and King Henry. "Now, Your Grace, what is it you ask of me?" One of her ladies brought the king a sweet cake and motioned him up to the throne.

Bishop Ward took his place behind the throne. King Henry glanced from the bishop to the queen. He began to sweat. Bishop Ward cleared his throat, and when that did not prompt the king, he took drastic measures by stepping in front of him. "Your Grace, if I may help the king to verbalize his request?" Bishop Ward's voice was shaky.

Queen Aurora's eyes narrowed. *Why is Ward nervous unless he knows of Henry's request? I shall let this play out.* She raised her index finger to her crown and rubbed the Angelite disc. "Why, Bishop Ward, is he sick? He appeared fine a few moments ago with all the dancing." She was suspicious of what the king wanted of her with this sudden change in demeanor. Her eyes narrowed at the king, who hid behind the bishop now. Gone was the pompous, arrogant ruler. Though there were lines around his eyes, he seemed boyish and afraid.

"No," Bishop Ward said. "It is just ... his request is of a delicate nature, and the king can't bring himself to ask because he is wrestling with his own conscience."

Queen Aurora raised an eyebrow at him. "Well, now I am intrigued, but he must ask me himself if I am to consider his request."

Bishop Ward, ever the diplomat, lowered his voice. "My queen, perhaps King Henry would feel more comfortable if we took this to a more private setting." His gaze darted to the side exit.

"I do not want to give in to the arrogant human king, especially after his display," she whispered to Ward, scrutinizing the king of England over his shoulder.

"Please, Your Grace, he begged for this meeting. He said it has to do with a family matter, as a father."

Queen Aurora's head jerked back at Ward's words. *Curiosity wins out over my better judgment. Yes, Ward knows what is going on. I wonder what Henry promised him this time.*

Queen Aurora's face was expressionless as she observed the king. "Very well, Bishop Ward, I will grant your request for privacy. This one time. Make no mistake, I do not like my time wasted. King Henry has but a few precious moments to make his request. Afterward, I want his circus out of my court, am I clear?" She gestured for Ward to lean closer. "You and I will have a talk later, Bishop."

Bishop Ward bowed his head and looked at King Henry, waiting for him to kneel. When the king did not, Ward cleared his throat. The king knelt, and the bishop answered, "Yes, Your Grace."

The queen stood and walked behind the throne, where two large doors stood, bearing a triangle with a horizontal line bisecting the top half, creating a smaller triangle. The symbol was outlined in blue lace agate; the stone, with its light-blue bands striped with bright blues and milky-white cloud-like mixtures, were reminiscent of a warm summer sky. The door handles were seven-pointed stars. Each point held a different vibrant-colored crystal. The door shimmered as if stardust had been sprinkled on the wood. The guards needed both hands to grab the handles and open the heavy doors.

Queen Aurora's private meeting room was as lavish as the doors suggested. Each wall faced one elemental direction and had the elemental symbol carved into the embellished walls, complete with its coordinating power crystal. If you could tear yourself away from the bulwark, the ceiling depicting the night of the Shooting Star was the real masterpiece: illustrating the moment the Star took off, its climb against the twilight sky, and its inevitable crash. The artist had used clear quartz crystals to represent the nighttime stars. Flash-green labradorite symbolized the Shooting Star as it began its journey. Titanium quartz signified the Star once it reached its pinnacle. The iridescent colors reflected in the quartz provided the perfect accent against the fresco of deep lavenders and cobalt blues denoting the changing evening sky. As the Star fell, the crystal transformed into fire-yellow citrine to capture its brilliance igniting the night sky as it crashed. The backdrop of the Star's re-entry was set against a navy-blue sky painted in fresco with an inlaid raw blue topaz crystal. It was tragically beautiful.

In the middle of the room sat a dark wood table, the legs gnarled as if the table had grown right out of the floor. Woven together along the border of the tabletop were Fae faction symbols; the large loops and curves made it appear as though the factions' symbols held each other in a loving embrace. In each corner of the long, rectangular table was an elemental symbol, and in the center was the seven-pointed star inlaid with smoky quartz. At the head of the table was a smaller version of the queen's throne, along with two chairs on each side. Each of the chairs had an elemental symbol carved above the head—these were the bishops' chairs. A guard removed a bishop's chair and replaced it with an ordinary chair for King Henry. Queen Aurora took her place at the head of the table and dismissed the guards. She extended her hand for the two men to sit.

A few moments of silence passed. Queen Aurora drummed her fingers on the table. "I am waiting, King Henry. I have indulged your request for privacy."

The king got up and, in a flash, was by her side on bended knee with his head bowed, babbling incoherently.

Queen Aurora looked at Bishop Ward, her eyes and lips pinched. Bishop Ward attempted to interject, but she lifted her hand to silence her advisor. Aurora's face relaxed as she stroked King Henry's back, allowing him to ramble on for a moment. Eventually his breathing slowed, and he raised his head to her.

Her eyes softened. "Take a breath, Your Highness, and tell me what you need. Your distress is obvious. How can I help to ease your pain?" Her voice was a cool caress. King

Henry was close to fifty-four years old. Queen Aurora had first met him when he was eighteen, new in his monarchy, and she had never seen him like this. He had always been a proud king. Henry swallowed, the tears making his green eyes the deep color of tulip stems peeking out from the snow. This should have warned her; there was always ice behind Henry's motivations. King Henry turned into her hand for a second, savoring her touch.

"Tell me what weighs so heavy on your heart," Aurora prompted. Her voice was gentle.

King Henry finally spoke in a still voice. "Mine own daughter ... Mary."

"Is she ill?" Aurora was aware of the politics of England; while she was not involved as per the treaty, unless asked, the religious conflict between the Catholic Church and the Church of England was of direct interest to the Fae. With King Henry's break from Rome, her pagan followers still practiced free from persecution. King Henry was far too busy enjoying being "The Head of the Church" and a friend to the Fae. He did not have time to hunt down "pagan heretics" as the Catholics called her followers.

King Henry whimpered before he spoke. "Nay, the lady is not ill, though I wish the lady were. It would make it easier. I'm afraid my people love her more than me or my son Edward. At the hour of my death, and if Edward dies before an heir he bears, Mary will inherit the throne."

Queen Aurora shook her head. "Your Grace, I am not sure what you are asking of me or why. I am sure Edward will bear a son, and if he does not, why is it of consequence? If Mary ascends to the throne, I am sure she will make a fine ruler."

King Henry broke, showing signs of frustration; his voice was no longer soft, his knuckles turning white as he pounded on his legs. "Because the lady shall reunite Rome and England under papal law and undo everything I have done. Mine own legacy shall be gone. You wench! I want Mary dead. *Kill Mary.* That is what I am asking. Mary cannot be on my throne." His eyes burned in anger and pride, his voice echoing in the room.

Queen Aurora stood, and a fearsome gale blew King Henry backward, pinning him against the wall. Her turquoise eyes glowed green with power. Her hair came undone from its knot and swirled around her. As she stalked toward the helpless king, energy wings sprouted from her back. With each step, she rose from the floor. When she reached him, she was ten feet off the ground, her wings twice the size of her body. The wind whipped around the room, slapping King Henry's face, causing his eyes to water.

"You fool! You are an insignificant worm." She whispered the insult with a cold sneer. "You come to me and ask me to kill your own flesh and blood? You are a father! She accepted your pitiful declaration as head of the Church, and she has done everything to earn your love, even when you abandoned her! Because you have taken the time to gaze in the mirror to see your youth is gone, and you realize control is nothing more than an illusion, you seek to direct another human being's exit from your realm to exercise one last bit of your ego? How dare you!" Her chest heaved and her eyes narrowed. "Do you think your God would forgive you for such an act? Do you think you are *a man*? You can't even kill her yourself; you ask another to do it for you! I will not kill Mary. I do not involve myself in your small matters. Leave my court, King Henry, and never return. You are banished from the Court of Light."

With a wave of her hand, she released the king from the wind's grip and sent him tumbling to the floor. With no concern, Aurora floated away, then paused, smirking. A derisive chuckle rolled from the back of her throat .

King Henry's eyes locked on hers as he trembled from head to foot.

Aurora leaned down and traced the side of his cheek with the back of her left index finger, caressing him like a lover. He flinched and she paused mid-stroke, tilting her head in warning. He squeezed his eyes shut as her finger twirled in the bristly hairs of his ginger beard, but she waited until his shoulders relaxed before she spoke, her voice silken. "One last bit of advice, Henry." He opened his eyes. She grabbed his chin, holding his face in place. He squirmed and begged. She smiled like a panther ready to consume its prey, teeth bared. "Don't even think about touching my followers in retaliation. If you do, I will see it as an act of war against the Fae. I will come for you, Henry, and whatever loved ones you hold dear. There will be nowhere for you to go and no one to protect you. Not your Church or your God. My army is bigger, and you can't hide from the elements. Get out of my sight." She pushed him away from her and stood. Henry said nothing, but tears streamed down his face. He drew the sign of the cross upon his breast and mumbled prayers.

Queen Aurora held her arms up, her wings and eyes blazing with the full fury of a wild storm. "Guardians, I call thee. Take Henry Tudor and revoke his invitation from me. So mote it be!"

The four walls representing the elements radiated their colors through the room, and the Guardians materialized in front of their respective stations. They descended upon King Henry, swallowing him up, and in a flash of brilliant red, blue, yellow, and green: he was gone.

Next, Queen Aurora addressed Bishop Ward. "Make sure the humans he brought are returned to their kingdom." Ward turned to leave, but Aurora was not finished with him. "Oh, and Bishop Ward?"

The bishop stopped with his hand on the door handle, his brow sweaty. "Yes, Your Grace?"

"Do not think I am unaware of your behavior, Ward? You are no longer emissary to England. You have clearly allowed yourself to be bribed by that buffoon. What did he promise you?"

Ward took two long strides toward his queen, bowing several times. "Nothing, Your Grace, I swear! I did not know what the nature of his inquiry was."

She held her hand up. "Silence!" The bishop winced, his golden ponytail swinging. "Henry is the epitome of what the war cost us. The humans have become egotistical and have strayed from the old ways. I know the bishops have allowed many of the English royals to buy our favor with their trinkets and land. We do not accept gifts for our time. If I discover you or any of the bishops are continuing to trade in favors, I will throw you to the Draconians. Don't you have a niece to take care of? Now go!"

Ward nodded. "Yes, Your Grace and Thank you for allowing me to have Indiga here. Ungarra has been most helpful with tending to-"

"Go."

Ward exited. Queen Aurora straightened her clothing, smoothing her hair. There were more people to receive. A queen's job was never done.

Chapter Three:
A Gift

M abon took place on the autumnal equinox; it was a celebration of light and dark when night and day were equal. The Court of Light would celebrate in peace. An Oracle reading took place at the Archway of Apala without incident. However, the reading mentioned that "bridges could be burned or built with blood or tears over troubled waters of fears. Sacrifices of a moon and a swan could be born from triumph, not tragedy, with a glance."

The prophecies were tricky, either very straightforward or a puzzle wrapped in a riddle. Aurora brushed it off; she could deliberate the meaning later, but today she had to figure out the issues with Queen Mary.

After King Henry VIII's banishment from the Court of Light, Queen Aurora kept a close eye on England's political affairs. Her threats had resonated with the king; he had left her pagan followers alone and did not seek revenge for his embarrassing exit from her court.

King Henry VIII passed on from this life on January 28, 1547, a year after his expulsion. As he hoped, his son

Edward inherited the throne. Edward was ten years old and very impressionable. It was clear his father had used his last year to hammer into his son his own values rather than teaching the young boy the skills he might need to serve as king.

As for his half-sisters, Princess Mary and Princess Elizabeth, King Edward declared them illegitimate, naming his cousin Lady Jane Grey the next in line of succession. King Edward died from tuberculosis in 1553, and his cousin lasted only nine days as queen before she was convicted of treason and beheaded. King Henry's worst fears became reality. The people proclaimed Mary the rightful ruler of England in July 1553. As Henry had foretold, Mary's first order of business was to begin the arduous process of reuniting Rome with England.

Queen Mary now had Queen Aurora's attention. While the Holy Father in Rome was a friend of the Fae, not all of his cardinals were, and Aurora needed to know precisely which side of the line Mary sat on. Mary had already begun hunting down Protestants. Aurora couldn't allow her followers to get caught up in this mess. An alliance with the royal family of England would be necessary, yet again.

Queen Aurora summoned Bishop Awynn to her private meeting room to discuss the matter. When she heard his footsteps rounding the corner, she opened the heavy ornate doors with a casual flick of her wrist and a gust of wind. Bishop Awynn stood in the doorway. He was the youngest of the bishops, but Queen Aurora enjoyed his optimism and fresh outlook on human matters. With his silver-white shoulder-length hair and his stark white uniform, he was a walking contradiction. His elemental faction was Fire. The single clue to the heat burning under the icy façade were his copper eyes—that and his staff made of ash and yellow topaz, both materials being Fire elemental amplifiers.

Queen Aurora walked over to greet her bishop. "Merry Meet, Bishop Awynn."

Bishop Awynn bowed. "Merry Meet, Your Majesty." A sweet, genuine smile reached his glittering eyes.

Aurora inhaled as the scent of cinnamon, cedar, vanilla and burning leaves filled the room. The scent often accompanied Fire Drake. She closed her eyes and enjoyed the sweet and spicy aroma.

Bishop Awynn's tone reminded her they were here to discuss business. "You asked to see me, Your Grace?" A subtle tilt of his head accentuated his smile.

Queen Aurora blushed. "Forgive me, Bishop Awynn. I always find your Fire Drake scent intoxicating. Yes, I asked for you because of the developments regarding England's new ruler, Queen Mary."

Now it was Bishop Awynn's turn to redden. Fire Drakes did give off an intoxicating scent, but it was for defense. The scent masked the sulfur odor which preceded the Fire Drake's fatal fireball. "I am honored you enjoy my scent, Your Grace. Yes, I am aware of the change in the monarchy. I have recently spoken to my priestesses. They told me of Queen Mary's triumphant march into London. If I recollect, they said she wore a purple velvet gown and a kirtle of purple satin decorated in pearl—so beautiful it would have made the heavens cry. She echoed the regal stature of her grandmother Queen Isabella of Spain. Her people believe her to be the rightful monarch of England."

Queen Aurora spun Bishop Awynn's account in her mind, searching for clues to her next move. "A purple gown, you say?"

"Yes, Your Grace. Is it of significance to you?" His mouth quirked as he leaned in a bit, angling his left ear toward his queen.

"Not to me. However, to the new queen of England, it may very well be." Aurora lifted her eyes to meet Awynn's, a glint of mischief visible.

"Bishop Awynn, do you know when her coronation ceremony is to be held?"

"Tomorrow."

"Interesting. I do not have much time." Aurora rubbed her hands together.

Bishop Awynn studied her face. "Your Majesty? Not much time for what?" This time there was a slight furrow to his brow.

Aurora smiled. "To find the new queen the perfect gift, of course!"

She thanked Bishop Awynn for his counsel and dismissed him, then paced, her wrists spinning in small, graceful motions. She balanced her Chakras, performing a moving meditation. Her steps were quiet and methodical as her hand motions became grander and more fluid. As a Sylph, Aurora could call the wind and ask it to deliver an Air crystal, the very crystal she now sought. But the spell would take concentration and an offering of energy.

Aurora took a deep, deliberate inhale. Then, closing her eyes, she exhaled and opened them; they flashed green. She was ready. She pivoted and waved her hand over the sparkling drapes covering the far back wall of her private meeting room. A breeze swept through the room, turning the pages of books lying open on the table. The candle's flames flickered, and the curtains dissipated, revealing two immense rose quartz crystal doors that opened as they solidified. The doors were faceted like diamonds, but opaque, with veins of white running through them.

Aurora passed over the threshold to the rose quartz balcony, making her way onto the terrace. It cracked and broke away from the castle. She would take the rose quartz with her to act as an amplifier, charging her energy on the way to her destination. Aurora's feet melded to the floor, merging with it. Her energy wings materialized, and the balcony suspended itself in the air, detached from the rest of the structure. Aurora lifted her hands, palms up, and closed her eyes. Her wings glowed brightly, the light suffusing from her wings, to her feet, and pooling onto a small puddle on the balcony. Then the radiant light spread to the entire quartz balcony. The structure was now a burning fireball of fuchsia streaking through the sky, carried by Aurora's sheer prowess. As she concentrated, a peaceful upturn of her lips softened her face.

The air stream passing by her ears sounded like the ocean crashing into the shore. Thoughts of Serena flooded her mind. She could see her rainbow tail and hear her laughter while the wind at the ocean was loud in her head. Aurora could feel her chakras spinning and lighting up. Her wings grew as Serena's laughter mixed with the wind, creating a melodic symphony of love and light. The Fae collective sang in her heart and in her Magick,

"I hear you, my friend; I miss you."

It was not a long flight, far too short for Aurora's taste; she could spend all day flying. She found her spot, and with a gentle hand motion, set the quartz balcony down by a meadow. With another undulating wrist gesture, her feet were released from the balcony, and she exited where the doors had once been. Feeling balanced and charged, she was prepared for what lay ahead.

Aurora scanned the area and spotted the small stream and field of English lavender she had seen from the air. The meadow held different hues of purple ranging from violet to lilac with hints of baby blue and sparkle pink. The breeze caressed the tops of the lavender flowers, creating a wave effect, mimicking the way the wind played over water. Orange and vermilion strokes of sunlight peeked through the trees. She inhaled the lavender flowers⬚ sweet scent and guided her hands over the petals as she walked through the meadow, savoring the heady fragrance. Lavender was a sacred flower to the Fae, and a useful essential oil. They used it to help humans relieve headaches, insomnia, tension, and stress. This was the perfect setting for her plan.

Several hours later, Queen Aurora sat in the meadow, playing with the tall blades of grass as fatigue settled into her bones. She held the beautiful crystal in her right hand, lifting it up to the fading sun. There was enough light to play off the deep saturation of aubergine at the tip. The color ran the gamut from plum to lilac until it became milky white at the base. Queen Aurora closed her eyes, lifted her chin, and stood. As she raised her arms, a slight breeze whistled through the meadow, and she gradually opened her eyes. In a sharp gesture, Aurora dropped her arms, energy traveling from her body out into the entire meadow in a flash of white light followed by a burst of blue, red, and green. The bright energy moved through every plant and creature occupying the meadow. The flowers bloomed, the trees grew exponentially, and the animals pranced. Queen Aurora voiced her gratitude over the fields:

"*Guardians of the East: Air. Your queen gives you blessings for your help today. I return the energy from whence it came; I give more than I take. Blessed be.*

"*Guardians of the South: Fire. Your queen gives you blessings for your help today. I return the energy from whence it came; I give more than I take. Blessed be.*

"*Guardians of the West: Water. Your queen gives you blessings for your help today. I return the energy from whence it came; I give more than I take. Blessed be.*

"*Guardians of the North: Earth. Your queen gives you blessings for your help today. I return the energy from whence it came; I give more than I take. Blessed be.*"

Queen Aurora stepped back when she was done, weary from the energy output. She would need time to recover before she could carry herself home. But when she glanced around at the effects of giving back to the meadow, she was happy to be tired.

After returning to the Court of Light, she sent word to Hogal, her metalworker. He was one of the few left of his faction, and a true artist concerning crystal and metalwork. Hogal had disheveled grey hair sticking out from under a red beanie. He stood four feet tall and wore chainmail overalls. His creased face showed all the hardships of someone who had survived the Fae wars. He had witnessed most of his lineage fade away. Once, his ancestry had been worshiped as the godly iterations of Vulcan and Hephaestus; now it was up to him and two other apprentices to carry on the legacy. Hogal greeted the queen with an honorable bow. He believed in formality with her, but she skipped protocol and hugged him. She regarded Hogal as a friend.

The crotchety Gnome squirmed and shook his head as he waved a finger at her. "Nots becoming of a queen," he teased.

She laughed. Aurora adored needling Hogal. He was salty, but they had a mutual understanding of the affection between them. "I have brought you a special project."

Hogal's eyes lit up; the only thing he enjoyed more than their banter were projects. "A special assignment?" His eyes were wide and curious.

"Yes, for the new queen of England."

Hogal rubbed his hands together. "Shows me, shows me!" He danced in place. Aurora opened up the pouch to reveal the raw amethyst. "Ohhhhhh, gimme me!" he squealed.

She placed the crystal in his calloused hands. They looked like worn leather: creased and rough, with deep lines and faded scars. "You have free rein, but..." Aurora said, seeing the wheels turning in Hogal's head.

His eyebrows rose and his lips pursed. "But?"

Aurora smiled with an arched eyebrow. "But I need it as a piece of jewelry."

Hogal smiled. "Done!"

"As always, I knew I could count on you, my dear, sweet Hogal." Aurora bent down and removed his hat to kiss him on the head.

Hogal feigned annoyance, but she knew he loved it. The Gnome bowed, leaving with a spring in his step to render his creation.

Within a few hours, Hogal ran back down the long corridor and past the quartz-hewn throne room to Queen Aurora's private meeting chambers. He slid to a halt as the guards stopped him at the grand, glittering doors. Out of breath and unable to speak, Hogal placed his hands on his knees. The guards eyed the Gnome, befuddled by his sense of urgency.

"Gets out of the way. I on a mission for the queen!" he spat in a grumpy, yet commanding tone.

The guard with gold rings in his forehead and lavender skin smirked and lowered his face to the small Gnome. "Be gone, Troll. The queen is far too busy to look upon your ugly face and your trinkets."

Even with Hogal's reputation and talent, his looks and shorter stature still caused him to be confused with a Troll by the more judgmental Fae. This had become a problem in recent times, as the Earthborn Fae had not been schooled on what it was like before the Court of Light was established. It was a generational gap, one Hogal was happy to educate them on. He referred to these types of Fae as "pollen wisps" and felt they were weak, many not having gone through the abandonment or the war. He often would say, "Blow on them and theys gets carried away."

The other guard with large ram's horns narrowed his gaze at Hogal, nudging his friend. "You heard about him, right?" He jabbed his thumb in the metal Gnome's direction.

The lavender hued Fae shook his head, his gold rings jingling. "Nope."

"That's the metal troll who bonded with his ward after the abandonment, like the other Virtues. The problem was his ward encompassed the crystals of the Earth, so for over three hundred years he was part of the Earth. Frozen in suspended animation, he connected with the crystals and learned how to communicate through an unspoken language with the Earth. But his energy was not meant for that life, and it began to drive him insane. He eventually was able to return to a form that allowed him to speak. But now he talks funny. "

"He is that Troll?" the lavender guard asked, eyes wide. "It doesn't matter. The queen is too busy for him."

Hogal folded his arms, and a wry smile crossed his lips. "And don't forget me power became augm-augmen-well stronger, along with me artistry becoming that of legend." Hogal took a bow.

The guard shook his head again. "Hey, Troll, did you hear me? I said scat!"

"Oh really, yous think so?" He crooked his finger, motioning the lavender guard closer to him.

The guard looked back over his shoulder at his ram-horned partner with a quizzical expression, then returned his attention to Hogal. "Yes?" The guard leaned closer to the Gnome, putting his hands on his knees, yet still they weren't eye level, Hogal having to look up.

Hogal smiled and punched him square in the nose. "I ain't no Troll!" The guard's eyes rolled back into his head, and he dropped like a dragon getting its wings clipped. Metalworking for thousands of years had given Hogal hands and arms like an oak tree. The other guard's mouth fell open. The Gnome took advantage and kicked the guard between his legs, leaving him clutching his own royal jewels as he slid to the floor. "Yous could use some manners. I don't do trinkets. I is an artist!" He hopped over the two fallen guards, clicking his heels together with a jump and whistling with pride.

Hogal approached the doors and closed his eyes, feeling for the metal within. Without touching them, he gave a push of his hands; the hinges creaked, and the doors yawned open.

Queen Aurora stood on the other side, her hands on her hips, shaking her head at the Gnome. He shrugged as the guards groaned. She motioned for him to enter, and with a flick of her wrists, a draft shut the doors behind the two friends.

Queen Aurora took a seat and offered one to Hogal at her meeting table. With an exhale, she smiled. "I hope my guards are not seriously hurt."

Hogal cracked his knuckles. "No, but those guys be needing to learn a lesson 'bout respect. I happened to be the right teacher." He leaned back, placing his hands behind his head.

Queen Aurora popped an eyebrow at him. "Really? Well, I am grateful to you. Be happy Desdemona didn't see. She might have something to say about you teaching her guards. She prefers to be the professor. However, I am positive you did not come to discuss lessons in decorum. I take it you completed the task I set before you?"

Hogal swallowed hard. "Desdemona ain't here, right?" His gaze darted side to side.

Aurora tightened her mouth, but the edges of her lips quirked upward. "No, she isn't. Besides, I thought you weren't afraid of anyone, dear Hogal?"

Hogal straightened, throwing his shoulders back and tilting his chin high.

Aurora knew Desdemona could be a bit off-putting, and for some reason, Desdemona and Hogal had never gotten along. Aurora believed it to be a Power Angel thing. Desdemona thought about everything in the way of rank and protocol; she tended to take things critically. Hogal was a bit more laid back.

Aurora brought her hands to her lips, stifling her laughter at Hogal's brave front. "Well, brave Hogal. How about you show me your latest creation?"

Hogal grumbled, and his nostrils flared as he made himself comfortable again. Then his shoulders relaxed. He slid an intricately designed gold box across the table. The gold box had a filigree motif with cutouts of leaves and flowers delicately interwoven into a square. The high gleam of the polished gold caught the light at every angle. The details in the ivy leaves were so lifelike. It looked just like the same plant that climbed up the side of Queen Mary's castle.

Aurora stared, her lips parted. She glanced between Hogal and the box several times. *His attention to detail is awe-inspiring.*

With her index finger and thumb, she lifted the top of the box, her heart pounding in anticipation. If this was just the vessel, she could only imagine what treasure it held.

Aurora caught her breath, opening the lid. Hogal had continued the same ivy filigree design on the brooch in an elaborate sunburst layout and in the center was the amethyst. He had faceted and polished the crystal to give it a luxurious gemstone quality anyone, human or Fae, would relish. Then he had placed it in a square setting a bit higher than the filigree designs around it, setting off its magnificence. A clover design cut out around the square setting drew one's eye straight to the sparkling stone; there was no mistaking the craftsmanship of this piece. Aurora was speechless.

Hogal's gaze was intense as he awaited her response. He held his breath and moved to the edge of his seat, his hands gripping the side of his chair. She met his stare; the piece was too beautiful to disturb. Hogal's lips trembled, his eyebrows raised. If his work elicited a request for permission to touch, his job was complete. Hogal nodded.

Aurora lifted the brooch from the box, using both hands to cradle it. It was a work of art, and even more beautiful up close. The leaves looked as if they had been picked that morning and dipped in gold. Transfixed by Hogal's artistry, Aurora examined the piece from every angle. *He truly is a genius.*

Aurora gently laid the brooch in the box as if tucking a Little One into bed. She stood, moving beside Hogal, who attempted to stand, but Aurora stopped him. The queen e bowed to the Gnome. "Hogal, of the faction of Gnomes, I am humbled by your artistry. I bow to you as Queen Aurora. For I may control the wind, but you, my friend, are gifted far beyond my greatest powers."

Hogal was the one left speechless this time. He embraced his queen with a hug, resting his cheek on her shoulder. Finally, the right words found him. "Thank you," he whispered.

After Hogal departed, Queen Aurora wrote a special note. She placed the note and the gift together on her window. Aurora briefly closed her eyes, calling the wind. The room filled with a warm current; a second later, the note and gift were gone. Aurora opened her eyes, *Enjoy your brooch, Your Highness. I am sure we will see each other very soon.*

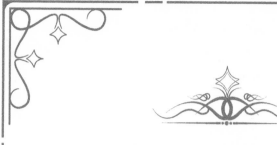

Chapter Four:
ALL HAIL QUEEN MARY
OF ENGLAND
(OCTOBER 1, 1553)

The crackling and popping of the dying fire provided the perfect ambient noise for the slight woman with strawberry-blond hair to gather her thoughts.

She sighed as she sat in her privy chamber, recalling the events of the last few days. She had managed to organize a coup, reunite with her half-sister, and depose the cousin who had tried to usurp her rightful place as queen of England. Many had tried to break Mary, and all of them had failed.

She made her way to the window, gazing at the stars, whispering, "Mother, the one and only queen of England I have ever known. I hope thou art proud of me today. I sought to bring dignity and honor back to thee." The woman bowed her head in prayer. A breeze broke her concentration, caressing her cheek.

"Mother?" Her voice was hushed as she wiped away pensive tears, the moment of reflection replaced with suspicion. Her heart thumped against her chest. The blood whooshed in her ears. She stood, scanning the empty room, clutching the rosary tucked inside her waist belt. A reflection from the stone windowsill caught her eye. The woman looked around, leery of the glittering gold box that now sat there. She approached slowly, and her fingers reached for the box but pulled back more than once as if worried that it was scalding. Balling her hands into fists, she paced and watched it, rubbing her cheek.

After an hour of contemplation, she blessed herself and stalked back over to the box. On the parchment on top of it, her name was written in beautiful calligraphy: "Queen Mary." Her fear subsided as the title rang in her head. *Queen Mary.* While she had heard it all day after the coronation, seeing it like this was different—special. Mary ran her hand carefully along the light-pink wax seal, which she did not recognize. But the seven-pointed star tugged at a recollection from her childhood like a lost memory cast deep into a river, and glimpsing the symbol had pulled at the thread. She struggled to retrieve a story her father had told her when she was a child. Mary remembered her father entertaining her with tales of sparkling people who lived far away in a gleaming castle, but those were children's bedtime stories.

She broke the seal, the scent of sage filling her nose as she unfolded the paper to read the note:

Your Grace, Queen Mary of England, the one true monarch:

Greetings. I am most happy to see the rightful heir sit on her throne. I wish your reign to be prosperous for all of England. I present you with this gift; it is an amethyst crystal from the Archangel Zadkiel, who is the Angel of forgiveness, grace, tolerance, and transformation of negative into positive energies. The crystal will help to calm and balance you as you rule. Should you ever be in need of service, light a fire and whisper these words into the night air:

Dearest Fae queen, sight unseen,
May I speak to a mentor, please
May he appear to me tonight,
So mote it be.

My most trusted advisor Awynn will appear to you, and he will carry your wishes to me personally, by my truth.

Fare thee well,
Queen Aurora, Queen of the Court of Light

Chapter Five:
A Moot Point

Neither Queen Aurora nor Bishop Awynn received word from Queen Mary for many moons, almost a year. Queen Mary acted on her word and had begun to sow the seeds, bringing England back into the folds of papal law and Rome. During this time, Bishop Awynn functioned as the ambassador to the Fae followers, both Light and Dark, assuring them a safe haven for religious rites and ceremonies in the area even as the changes swept over England. Aurora had very few dealings with King Jarvok during this time. But in the spirit of full disclosure, she did see that Bishop Awynn kept King Jarvok's lieutenants abreast of the developing situation. The Dark Fae had been quiet since the treaty signing, following the stipulations set forth: they stayed on their side, and Aurora made sure her kin kept to theirs.

Fearing Queen Mary might turn on her pagan followers, Aurora called a council to discuss the matter. Queen Aurora took her place at the head of the table and welcomed her bishops to take their seats. One by one they did, by seniority: Bishop Geddes, Bishop Ward, Bishop Caer, and last, Bishop Awynn.

"Merry Meet, my friends," she addressed the eclectic group sitting before her.

"Merry Meet, Your Grace," the Fae replied in unison, all bowing their heads.

"I ask for your guidance in the matter of England, more specifically Queen Mary. She has begun laying the foundation to reunite England under papal law, bringing back the humans' strict interpretation of what they call Catholicism or the Word of God." She rolled her eyes, and the bishops chattered a bit among themselves.

Bishop Geddes spoke up first. His steely gaze focused on the stained-glass window as he cupped his chin. He stroked his goatee. "Your Grace, we have strong relations with His Holiness. If Queen Mary does reunite England with Rome, we can speak with His Holiness. I believe she would listen to his word above all others. He could explain why a relationship with us is so important and why leaving certain followers alone is in her best political interest."

Aurora sat back in her chair, her gaze flicking side to side.

Bishop Geddes' impatience got the best of him. "Perhaps we could reveal our true origin to her. If she knew we were Ang—"

A gust stole his breath and pinned him to his chair.

Aurora stood, her energy wings growing. Their fuchsia glow bounced off the Quartz crystal walls, causing the others to look away. Their brilliance could cause blindness.

"NEVER!" she shouted hoarsely. Her neck flexed with tension. "We are Fae!" The wind picked up in intensity. Books, candelabras, and vases flew about the room in a frenzy, smashing against the walls. Aurora's eyes, a dazzling shade of jade, blazed with power and rage at the bishop's blasphemous suggestion. "WE ARE FAE! DO I MAKE MYSELF CLEAR?" She glared at each bishop until they nodded their comprehension.

The wind died down, and the objects caught up in her whirlwind dropped to the floor; the sound of breaking crystal and ceramic muffled by the cyclone of her gradually diminishing temper.

"Get out. You are dismissed," she said, her tone cool.

Each bishop bowed and took their leave. Bishop Awynn was the last, due to his rank, and as he walked past the window, he paused with a shudder.

"What is it, Bishop Awynn?" Aurora rested her forehead on her fingertips.

Bishop Awynn offered her a small grin. His eyes glinted like fireflies at midnight. "Your Grace, this meeting might have been moot." His smile grew larger, and he tilted his head upward as if listening to a distant melody.

Aurora looked at the bishop, not sure if she was angry or intrigued. "What?" She squinted.

Bishop Awynn stood tall, pulling his shoulders back.

Aurora's brow furrowed. "Where is your newfound confidence coming from, Bishop?"

"It seems Queen Mary has just summoned me. With your permission, my queen, I should not keep Her Majesty waiting."

Chapter Six:
An Introduction (March 1554)

Queen Mary paced her chamber, speaking in a hushed, frenetic voice. There was no one in her privy chamber—she had kicked them all out before tearing apart her room searching for the gilded box and note. It had taken her hours before she found it hidden behind a loosened stone near her bedside table. She exhaled in relief when she recovered it. The box was extraordinary; she stared at it, lost in the detail of the ivy leaves, which reminded her of the castle in Greenwich. Now that she had completed the instructions from the note, she waited. "Where art thou?"

Air whipped from the fireplace, blowing a few stray hairs from her face. The woman gaped at the hearth, clutching her rosary. The air shimmered, a flame leaped out from the hearth, and a man rose from the blaze.

"By the Devil's own! Get away, demon!" She dropped to her knees, gesturing the sign of the cross, rubbing the beads of her rosary between her fingers as she muttered the prayers.

Bishop Awynn fully materialized, unsurprised by Queen Mary's white and ghoulish complexion. "No, Your Majesty. I am Bishop Awynn, last of the Fire Drake Faction of Fae. I represent Queen Aurora, ruler of the Court of Light. I heeded your call, and I am here." He gave a long, low bow to the praying woman.

Tremors ran through Queen Mary's body, and she remained on her knees, clutching the cross. "Thou art not a demon?" Her voice trembled, and she did not meet his eyes.

"No, Your Majesty, I am not. I am a ward of the element of Fire. If I may demonstrate to ease your mind?"

Queen Mary nodded, slowly rising to her feet but keeping her distance.

Bishop Awynn waved his hand in a circular motion, and a flame from the fireplace traveled in a ribbon of oranges, reds, and yellows to snake up his arm and land in the palm of his hand. Awynn closed his hand around the flame and opened it to reveal the shape of a dove. The flame dove pecked at his hand and flapped its wings. The queen scrutinized the "bird," taking a few slow steps closer. Bishop Awynn closed his hand, and with another gesture, the ribbon of flames traveled back to the fireplace.

Queen Mary clapped her hands. "Sire, thou art a most wondrous magician." Her face glowed with genuine amusement.

Bishop Awynn smiled. "Thank you, Your Majesty. You are far too kind." He extended his hand.

She hesitated but gently placed her small, soft hand in his. Her touch lingered in his palm for a moment, and she tilted her head, *curious*. "My, 'tis warm." Queen Mary gave the bishop a coy smile as he brought the back of her hand to his lips. The bishop's lips felt cool compared to his hand, which had just played with the fire dove. She inhaled and exhaled slowly, her tension unwinding along with her apprehension.

Awynn stepped back and gave her a gracious, deep bend as he announced himself. "Bishop Awynn, Fourth Advisor to the Court of Light under the reign of Queen Aurora, at your service."

Queen Mary curtsied out of respect. "Greetings, Bishop Awynn. 'Tis a pleasure to make thy acquaintance. Welcome."

"How may I be of service to you?"

Queen Mary wrung her fingers and paced. Bishop Awynn watched her intense movements. She pulled at the threads on her white lace sleeves but switched back to wringing her fingers. Finally, Queen Mary stopped and faced the bishop. "Bishop Awynn, I need to know I can trust thee," she pleaded.

Bishop Awynn placed his hand over his heart. "Yes, Your Majesty, you have my word."

"Prithee take me to the Court of Light. I will speak with Queen Aurora myself, and I shall beseech mine own truth." Determination mounted on her face.

Bishop Awynn respected the new monarch's grit, but he was not at liberty to grant her an audience without discussing this with his queen. "Queen Mary, I will take your request to Queen Aurora and return tomorrow eve with an answer."

The queen exhaled in relief, and her shoulders slumped. "Promise thou shalt return?" The pleading look had returned for a moment.

"You have my word, Your Majesty. Fae are bound by our word. We do not lie." He stepped back to the fireplace.

With a raise of his staff, the flames enveloped him, and Bishop Awynn vanished.

Queen Mary dropped to her knees and began to pray.

Bishop Awynn reappeared in a meadow outside of London where his horse waited. He morphed into a man with flowing orange hair and a halo of gold: he was Belenus, the Celtic sun god. He needed the form to approach the fire attended by one of Belenus's most trusted followers. In London, fire did not exist in its natural state, like an erupting volcano, so he required some assistance to jump the Veil. He had called upon a priestess to keep a bonfire lit to act as his portal.

The Fae traveled back and forth through the Veil via the Oaken Doorway. The Bishops could travel through the Oaken Doorway through their connection to their elements in their innate condition once on the human side of the Veil, while other Fae needed an elemental crossroads—the meeting of two elements such as Earth and Air or Water and Earth—to open the doorway. The bishops' synergistic relationship with their elements provided one other gift: they could travel short distances in the human world by riding the energy of their element. Awynn was lucky Queen Mary kept a fire burning in her privy chamber; by making a small fire outside her castle, he was able to concentrate on her call and ride the energy, using her fireplace to pull him to her.

The sweet scent of cedar and leaves filled the air as the smoke billowed above the treetops. Awynn tapped his horse's sides to hurry him along.

Once he reached the portal, he dismounted his white mare and kissed the priestess on the cheek. She bowed without a word. Awynn closed his eyes and searched the trees to make sure he could not sense any other humans close by. Assured he was alone, he raised his staff and spun it. The flames from the bonfire created a ring of fire. He walked toward the spiraling flames, his Celtic god façade disintegrating, and spread his palms to part the flames. Bishop Awynn stood unfaltering and composed in the fiery circle. He was majestic amid the heat and blaze. This was where he felt most comfortable wielding this power. He was the calm in commotion, the serenity in anarchy. He allowed the tranquility of it to seep into his bones as he chanted, "South frees Fire: the flame roars; open my door: allow me home once more. So mote it be."

A door outlined in flames appeared, and Awynn walked through as the swirling flames dissipated. A moment later, he emerged through a door in an oak tree outside the Court of Light's castle. He moved fast through the palace, finding his way to Queen Aurora's private meeting room where the other three bishops waited for him with the queen. The room was thick with anticipation. The bishops sat fidgeting.

"Merry Meet, Bishop Awynn. I take it you have information to report?" Queen Aurora gestured for Bishop Awynn to take a seat.

"Merry Meet, Your Highness, my fellow bishops. Yes, I have met with Queen Mary." Bishop Awynn took a quick look around, trying to figure out how to phrase Queen Mary's request for an audience.

"Well ... get on with it." Bishop Geddes' frustration was palpable.

Queen Aurora flicked her wrist, and a gust of wind blew the bishop's staff over and closed the book he had open.

Bishop Geddes turned to Queen Aurora. "Forgive me, Your Grace." He had the sense to look chagrined.

Aurora stared at the bishop. "Do not test me, Bishop Geddes. Continue, Bishop Awynn. What did Her Majesty Queen Mary need?"

Bishop Awynn swallowed and found his voice; he knew there was no sense prolonging it. "Queen Mary humbly requests an audience with Your Grace to present her case in person." He bowed but wasn't sure why he felt like he should, given the nature of the news he had delivered.

The table erupted in protests from the other bishops, but Queen Aurora relaxed back in her chair, stroking her bottom lip. She leaned her elbow on the armchair's rest.

"Your Grace, a Tudor has not been in the Court of Light for years," Bishop Ward reminded the queen.

"Shouldn't we make Queen Mary wait a bit, not be so accessible? If you see her so soon, it will look like we are bending to *her* will," Bishop Geddes advised.

"Enough!" Her turquoise eyes tightened, flashing green for a moment. The table fell silent. "Bishop Awynn, I am most pleased with how you have served the court today. Tomorrow night, you will escort Queen Mary here for a private audience with me in the Great Hall." Queen Aurora's face relaxed, and she tapped her chin.

"Your Grace, I told Queen Mary I would give her an answer tomorrow night. What if she is not prepared to come with me on such short notice?"

Aurora was already one step ahead of Awynn, writing a note as he asked his question. Folding a piece of paper, she glided to the window and whispered into the night air, "A whisper in the wind doesn't last long; it soon disappears, and then it is gone." The cool wind snatched the paper from Aurora's hand. She watched it as it soared on the currents like a butterfly until it vanished.

Queen Aurora stretched her hands on the table, splaying her fingers and flattening her palms. She lifted her chin and made eye contact with each of the Fae at the table, then calmly laid out her instructions. "Queen Mary has been made aware of the plans for tomorrow evening. She will be waiting for you, Bishop Awynn. I have instructed her to call for you when she is ready. You will bring her to the Great Hall, and I will listen to her request. She will be granted safe passage to and from the Court of Light."

Bishop Awynn spoke up, his hand over his heart. "Yes, Your Grace." The other bishops followed in unison.

"You are dismissed. Until tomorrow's eve, gentle Fae."

Chapter Seven:
SINS OF THE FATHER
(MARCH 1554)

The night sky swallowed the light of day. Bishop Awynn waited patiently by the Oaken Door for Queen Mary's call. The message came to him on the backs of fireflies in a sweet, familiar song, a low hum meant solely for his ears. With a thought and a shimmer, Belenus emerged. He stepped into the Oaken Doorway, materializing in the meadow outside of London. As planned, a pagan priestess waited for him with a white horse and a roaring fire.

"Thank you, my child. Please tend to the fire until I return; when the flames change to blue, you will know I am near, so make yourself scarce... I will reward you for your loyalty."

The young woman bowed. "Yes, Great Belenus."

Awynn kissed her cheek and mounted his horse. His cult was plentiful and strong here. It was in his best interests for this relationship with Queen Mary to be mutually beneficial; it keep them all safe. As the Celtic god, he wore a gold sunburst crown with long, flowing orange hair. His skin remained luminescent, but his build was more muscular, his ears pointed, and his eyes looked like molten orbs of lava. His staff was a spear, and his uniform of white became gold with a dark-green velvet cape. He sensed some of his followers watching his remarkable form leave the meadow.

Once through the trees, well out of sight, Awynn shook off Belenus' identity. With a kick to the sides of his white steed, he made haste to see Queen Mary.

Outside the castle, Awynn tied his horse to a tree and started a small fire with flint rock and dried grass. Concentrating on Queen Mary's call, he balanced his Chakras, and with a brusque inhale, his body had no form, becoming the stillness in the center of every flame, the white-hot embers igniting the fire. With a rush of air, Bishop Awynn felt himself congealing. The power, the heat, the separation, being pulled apart, only to be rebuilt again! *What a strange dichotomy*, he thought. *This sensation never gets any easier.*

Then Bishop Awynn was once again flesh and blood, standing in front of Queen Mary's hearth.

Queen Mary's eyebrows rose at his sudden appearance, her delicate hands covering her lips. "Bishop Awynn, I am pleased to see thee again. How shall we travel to the Court of Light?" Her hands dropped to reach for her skirt as if she had remembered her manners, and she curtsied.

Bishop Awynn noticed the gifted amethyst brooch and smiled. *Queen Mary is shrewd if nothing else.* "It is a pleasure to see you again, Your Majesty. I have a horse just outside the castle walls. We will travel to a special passageway only I can open, but you must trust me. Do I have your trust, Your Highness?" Bishop Awynn bowed and extended his hand to her.

Queen Mary's lips curled in a coquettish grin as she looked up at him through her pale eyelashes. "Aye, thou hast my trust. We must be careful as we leave, for my guards cannot see us together. Follow me, dear Bishop Awynn. I know a way out of the castle." She motioned for him to follow as she opened her door and checked the hallway. Queen Mary spoke in a hushed voice. "I did as thy queen asked and told my guards and ladies to grant me privacy tonight. I remember sneaking 'round these stairs as a babe."

There was an air of mischief in her voice. Awynn grinned at the affinity for harmless trouble Mary appeared to have. It reminded him of the stories he had heard about Queen Aurora and her best friend, Lady Serena.

The two ran down the back stairs and out the servants' kitchen. A few of the kitchen help spotted them but were so busy bowing and kneeling, the two were gone before anyone could get a good look at the Fire Drake. They jumped on Awynn's white steed and made off into the trees, Queen Mary giggling like a little girl for the entire ride. Awynn wondered if this was the first time she had laughed in years.

Once they were a few horse's lengths from the meadow, Awynn flicked his hand, turning the roaring fire bright blue. As they came to the clearing, the blue fire illuminated the meadow in gorgeous hues of cerulean, indigo, and sapphire.

Bishop Awynn helped Queen Mary dismount, for she was far too busy staring open-mouthed at the tranquil blue flame dancing in front of her. The fire cast a glow on her pale skin, making her complexion similar to Awynn's own otherworldly luminescence.

Mary raised her hands to her lips. "By all which is holy, 'tis most wondrous."

Bishop Awynn bowed. "Thank you, Your Majesty, but now I must concentrate on opening the portal. Once I do, you must trust me, without hesitation." His voice was gentle but with underlying conviction.

Queen Mary nodded and stepped back, folding her hands together. It was not a submissive gesture by any means.

Bishop Awynn swirled his staff as he had done many times when creating a ring of fire. He stepped toward the flames and spread his palms to part them. Then he called for Queen Mary to take his hand. She looked at the spinning ring of fire and took a deep breath. *I have faced rebellions and Anne Boleyn, this will be nothing for me,* she thought. Queen Mary tightened her mouth and squared her shoulders as she took Bishop Awynn's hand. Both of them stepped through the opening of the blaze to stand in the middle of the deafening madness.

Queen Mary studied the Fae inside the chaotic whirl of energy. He was preternaturally serene. *"South frees Fire: the flame roars; open my door: allow me home once more. So mote it be,"* he intoned.

Mary stretched her hand toward the flames. She expected blistering heat, yet there was none. Queen Mary grasped Awynn's hand tighter as a door outlined by flames appeared in the air. A soft tremble ran through her, and Awynn squeezed her hand for reassurance. He placed his hand on her back and guided her through the doorway.

Queen Mary closed her eyes at the last second, the rush of the inferno drowning out all sounds until there was silence.

Bishop Awynn and Queen Mary appeared through a door in an oak tree. Queen Mary gazed up at a castle unlike anything she had ever seen. Awestruck, she stood outside the Court of Light in the Veil of the Fae, one hand at her mouth and one upon her heart. Many animals milled about, none of them afraid of their presence, and Mary asked Awynn questions about each one. Even the grass shimmered and shone.

Bishop Awynn took her hand, leading her to a bridge spanning a lake so blue she could not even have dreamt of it if she tried. The rush of the waterfall to her right was melodic as it poured over cut rocks and boulders gleaming in the pale moonlight. Mary returned her attention to the blue water as it twisted and turned, but she balked at placing her foot on the bridge. Awynn nudged her, gently guiding her forward. She touched her toes to the bridge and jumped back, balling her fists up as she brought them up to her cheeks. Awynn allowed the human queen to compose herself and explore this strange new world. He took a few steps back, giving Mary the space she needed, his eyes gentle and soft as the small-framed woman gathered her layers of crinoline and took a deep breath in her restrictive corset. She knelt and examined the bridge. He watched her run her hands along the smooth grey surface with its rainbow veins. Tilting her head parallel to the bridge, she scrutinized every facet of the glittering marvel.

She did not look at Bishop Awynn as she spoke. "I have never seen this! Will it hold us?" Trepidation was thick in her voice.

Bishop Awynn stepped onto the bridge and jumped up and down to prove it would. The bridge lit up with each jump. "It is made of titanium quartz. Some call it flame aura, Your Majesty. It is one of the strongest crystals, and it recognizes me as a Fire Drake. It lights up when our energies come in contact."

Queen Mary smiled at his silly display, laughing at the wonderment of it all. He extended his hand to help the queen to her feet, and she grasped it with no qualms. The two walked across the crystal bridge.

At the gate, Queen Mary scanned it, perplexed by the shiny, dark slate metal. Bishop Awynn raised his staff, and its yellow topaz crystal began to glow brightly. "I am Bishop Awynn, Fourth Advisor to the Court of Light under the reign of Queen Aurora. I am accompanied by Queen Mary of England and Ireland. She is to have an audience with Queen Aurora. I request safe passage through the Hematite Gate. We bear no ill intentions. Do we have permission to enter?"

The guards above yelled down, "Merry Meet, Bishop Awynn. Please pass through."

As the ominous gates opened like the jaws of a giant serpent welcoming its prey, Queen Mary swallowed, clutching Awynn.

Once through the gates and inside the palace's courtyard, Queen Mary could see the entire castle was made of crystal. The center was not like her castle, for there was no market, no receiving area, and it was silent with clear vertical reflecting ponds. Mary watched the fish and other creatures she had never seen before swimming about. There were trees bearing fruit of gold and silver, not orange or red. The horses had tails the colors of the rainbow, like something from a child's dream.

Bishop Awynn took her toward the arches of the veranda. With so much to see and touch, Mary did not know where to look. Awynn hurried her through a doorway, and once inside, he guided her to a grand gilded staircase with a gold railing.

"The Great Hall is this way, Your Majesty. There will be a room for you to freshen up before you see Queen Aurora, if you'd like."

Queen Mary tried concentrating on Bishop Awynn, but the sights of the palace kept drawing her in. He repeated himself, and finally she understood his offer. "I thank thee." She had a lilt to her voice, as if trying not to sound too distracted.

At the top of the staircase, he opened a mahogany door carved with different symbols. Queen Mary's eyes scanned the symbols, her forehead crinkling as she raised her fingers to them, but she withdrew her hand. Bishop Awynn stepped aside to allow her to enter first. She gave Awynn a slight grin, glancing up at the door carvings as she passed him by. The room was large and circular, surrounded by floor-to-ceiling arched windows that allowed the silver moonlight to fill the room. The rays of moonlight bounced off the fluorite crystal floor, highlighting the ribbons of purple, green, white, and turquoise reflecting like waves on water. The rest of the room held opulent furniture made of velvet cushions with plush pillows and large stone vases overflowing with flowers. The walls and ceiling had murals depicting images of Mermaids and horses with glittering horns, both so realistic they might jump from the wall and land in your lap.

Queen Mary reached out to touch the image of the golden-haired Mermaid sitting on a rock surrounded by waves. The Mermaid's face held a glint of mischief, reminding Queen Mary of her half-sister Elizabeth. The queen lowered her eyes. She worried about Elizabeth and the rumors that her sister was involved in the revolts.

Bishop Awynn cleared his throat when he saw Queen Mary studying the floor. "The floor is made of fluorite, a wonderful stone to help calm and relieve anxiety, tension, and stress. It helps to detoxify the emotional body and mind. Queen Aurora had this room commissioned for her guests who have an audience with her, to help them gather their thoughts and soothe their minds. I will leave you to freshen up and prepare to see her. Should you need assistance just call and I will come." Bishop Awynn bowed.

Queen Mary curtsied. "I thank thee. Thou art most kind." She turned her attention toward the window.

Bishop Awynn left the queen to her thoughts and came upon the large carved doors of Queen Aurora's private chambers. He chuckled at the unusual angle of the nails as he recalled the story of Hogal's last visit. He knocked on his queen's door.

"Yes, Bishop Awynn, enter."

Seeing her dressed in royal garb always took Awynn's breath away. She was beautiful, even when she was not in her majestic attire. However, when she wore her receiving gowns, her brands were visible. The notion of Queen Aurora allowing her metalworking Gnome to brand her with the faction of each Fae line that had met their Oblivion both baffled him and deepened his respect for her.

She caught him staring at her back, their eyes meeting in the mirror's reflection. Without turning, she spoke. "Ask your question, Bishop Awynn." Her tone was flat.

Awynn averted his gaze, realizing his misstep. "Forgive me, Your Grace."

"There is nothing to forgive. I wouldn't have done this to myself if I didn't want them to be seen. Therefore, I will extend my invitation this one time. Ask your question."

"I have but one. Why? And did it hurt?" His eyes grew warm like a smoldering flame as he leaned forward.

Queen Aurora removed her crown and placed it on the vanity. *There is no room for royalty in this conversation.* «Technically, Bishop Awynn, you asked two questions, but I will indulge you. Please.» She extended her hand for him to sit. «My answer is simple. I am your queen. I was their queen too. She grazed the brands her spine with her thumbnail delicately. "It is my solemn honor to protect the Fae, no matter the cost, and I let them down. The war with the Court of Dark should have ended sooner. Had I chosen to negotiate with King Jarvok earlier, more Fae lives may have been spared. As queen, my kin come first— not ego, nor beating King Jarvok." Her eyes reflected hues of turquoise—unshed tears. "These factions will never grace the Earth again. Therefore, the few moments of pain I endured is nothing compared to their Oblivion. I must never forget them or the mistakes I made. I will never fail to remember how their sacrifice taught me how to be a better queen for all. To answer your other question, yes, it hurt. Before you ask, because I am sure the thought crossed your mind, the brand is inflicted with a metal template of the faction symbol. I would do it a thousand times again to bring back just one of these lines." Queen Aurora placed the crown on top of her head again, looking more like a queen than she had before their conversation.

"Your Majesty, you couldn't have stopped—"

"Bishop Awynn, you asked, and I answered. I am not looking for absolution or empathy. I know my shortcomings as a ruler. I have grown and will continue to. I will fall, but it is how I pick myself up and elevate those who support me. I make no excuses. Now, let's not keep the queen of England waiting."

Queen Aurora walked out, ready to meet her next test.

Queen Aurora took her place on her throne. She had called the Guardians, who were watching without a sound. Desdemona was well hidden in the geometric tiles of the ceiling; the last thing Aurora needed was her brash captain of the Illuminasqua frightening the new queen of England.

Aurora nodded to her guards, and they opened the majestic rose quartz doors to the Great Hall. Bishop Awynn stood, bowed, and extended his right hand. An attractive woman with strawberry-blond hair came into view: high cheekbones, thin lips, and a milky complexion. She wore her hair swept up under a cap of black velvet edged with small white pearls, and a petite gold veil trailed behind the cap, also edged in pearls to complete the delicate coif. Her dress was black and gold brocade with white trim along the neckline, and the sleeves were accented with the same delicate pearls as her cap. The bottom of the underskirt had a touch of the white trim, with gold thread to finish the hemline. At the center of her dress was Queen Aurora's amethyst brooch. The black and gold brocade offset the purple gemstone impeccably.

Aurora grinned, her hands folded on her lap as she watched the first queen of England enter the Great Hall.

Queen Mary took Bishop Awynn's hand graciously, and in true royal fashion glided toward the throne. There was no posing or grandstanding, unlike her father, King Henry VIII. Queen Mary was the personification of grace.

Bishop Awynn bowed again once he reached Queen Aurora's throne. "Queen Aurora, may I present to you Queen Mary of England and Ireland."

Bishop Awynn stepped aside to take his place next to Queen Aurora's throne. Queen Mary gave a deep and proper royal curtsy to Queen Aurora, waiting until Aurora gave her permission to rise.

"Welcome, Your Grace," Aurora said. "The Fae were most happy to hear of your rightful accession to the throne."

"I thank you with all my heart, Queen Aurora. Your palace is lovely." Queen Mary bowed her head.

Aurora nodded. "I am pleased to see you are wearing my gift. It looks exquisite on you."

Mary delicately brushed the brooch with her fingers. She looked up at Aurora through her lashes with a prim quirk of her lips. "I thank you, Queen Aurora. Your gift was very thoughtful." She gave another curtsy out of respect.

Yes, Mary is years ahead of her father in terms of manners. "Your time is most valuable, Queen Mary. I am sure the castle will miss you if I keep you too long. How may I help you?"

Mary's thin lips tightened, and she straightened her shoulders, the Tudor resolve kicking in. "Your Grace, my request is of a delicate nature."

Aurora's stomach clenched. It ended badly for the last Tudor who began their request in a similar fashion. But she leaned forward. "I am listening."

"I need help conceiving an heir for mine own betrothed, Prince Phillip of Spain. He is younger than I. I am afraid I shall not grant him a son. I want to please him and my state with an heir. Some do not approve of our marriage, and I believe an heir shall help calm the waters. I was told you can help me." Mary gave a hurried curtsy at the end of her request.

Queen Aurora leaned back in her throne, making her face unreadable to the English monarch as she deliberated. *It has taken all of Mary's strength and resolve to ask for help; she even forgot her manners for a brief second.* Queen Aurora pushed off her throne in a move of grace and urgency, her sudden shift causing her hair to fall from its loose bun down her back in a tumbling of crimson flames. To her credit, Queen Mary did not budge as the Fae queen approached her. Aurora held both her hands out to the new monarch, beckoning her to rise.

Mary's eyes went distant as she tilted her head and bit her lip before refocusing on Aurora's hands. "Hail, holy queen, mother mercy. Our Life, our sweetness, and our hope," Mary mumbled, repeating the prayer. "Do not be afraid, Your Highness. Take my hands," Aurora murmured softly.

Mary inhaled and gave a subtle shake of her head as she took Aurora's hands. Aurora felt her relax and smiled. "I will grant your request for help, Queen Mary, but I have conditions. They must be followed without exception."

Queen Mary let go and gave a deep curtsy. "I thank you. I thank you. I am eternally grateful."

Aurora took Queen Mary by her shoulders. "You are welcome, but first you should hear my terms before you agree. We ought to have an understanding, Your Majesty."

Mary nodded emphatically as Aurora stared into her eyes.

Aurora called for Bishop Awynn. "Please bring me a contract for a changeling exchange. See Lady Sekhmet for what is needed to complete Her Majesty's request."

Bishop Awynn bowed and left with exigency in his gait.

Queen Aurora returned her attention to Queen Mary. She gestured for them both to sit on the steps leading to her throne. "These are my terms, Your Grace. If you do not understand any part, please let me know. It is imperative that we enter into our agreement with complete comprehension."

"I understand. Please continue with your terms."

Bishop Awynn returned promptly with a roll of paper and handed it to Queen Aurora. She closed her eyes, waving her hand over the parchment, which shimmered and glowed as if it would catch fire.

Queen Aurora smiled. "Very well, listen carefully, Queen Mary of England and Ireland, for you have asked for my help in bringing you a child—an heir to your throne. You have my word as queen of the Court of Light: I will grant your request of a child. No more, no less."

Queen Mary swallowed as she sat listening with rapt attention.

"You will be with child by the third full moon after your wedding night. I will choose the father. He will be of Fae descent to ensure virility. I will send him to your bedchamber ten days after your monthly bleed once you are married. I will also give you a special tea to ensure your fertility. If the child you give birth to has the physical traits of the Fae, a changeling will be exchanged. This changeling will last for a few days and then expire. The other child will be taken away upon birth, raised as a Fae in the Court of Light, and you will have the opportunity to bear another child. This is not negotiable; you will never speak of the first child or ask to see him or her. In exchange for my help in procreating a child, I ask for the following.

"First, you will never speak of your time here in the Court of Light or your knowledge of the existence of the Fae. We are worshiped as gods and goddesses to help humanity; our true Fae forms are sacred. Very few humans, besides yourself, are privy to this knowledge. We guard our secrets with our lives and expect any human we help to respect our wishes.

"Second, you will allow the pagan priests and priestesses who are under Fae protection to practice without fear of persecution. No human who is practicing under any of our covens on behalf of our god or goddess personas are involved in witchcraft or acting in a malevolent manner with Fae blessings, I assure you. Leave them be. We are not responsible for plagues or any such nonsense. Do not feed into the paranoia. We govern our covens; we will police them, and we will deal with them. It is not up to you to intervene.

"Third, Queen Mary, you will personally leave a tribute for the Court of Dark on the winter solstice and the Court of Light on the summer solstice. And finally, you will never speak of this agreement or of the father of the child.

"However, should you break any of the rules I have set forth on this night, our covenant is null and void. My word will not bind to our deal. Breaking these rules will be seen as an act of war against the Fae. You will be banned from the Court of Light, and retribution will be mine to seek as I see fit. Should you break these rules while you are with child, the pregnancy will be terminated."

When Queen Aurora finished speaking, the paper levitated off the floor between the two queens; then it glowed, and a spectrum of soft lights emanated from it. Mary lifted a hand to shield her eyes from the brightness. The paper dimmed, floating to land between the monarchs. Mary gawked as what was once blank now contained the words Queen Aurora had just spoken.

Queen Aurora lifted her index finger and removed a blade of crystal from her gown. A quick swipe of the blade left a drop of blue liquid on her index finger. Queen Aurora used her finger to sign her name on the paper. "With my blood, I am bound to honor my word." She turned to Mary. "It is your turn, Your Grace. Do you understand the agreement? Do you agree to the terms I have set forth?"

Queen Mary pulled out the rosary she had tucked into her right sleeve. The crucifix was swallowed by her fist, her knuckles white with the pressure of her grip. Her thumb massaged the first bead, her lips moving as she recited the Lord's Prayer to herself. Aurora referred to these religious prayers as poems, and she was familiar with this one.

The English monarch shook her head to bring herself back to the present situation. She glanced up at Aurora and relaxed her grip on her faith's life raft. "What pagans are under your protection? How shall I know them?" Mary asked.

Queen Aurora respected her attention to detail. "My pagan followers worship several of the Fae as Celtic gods and goddesses. For example, Bishop Awynn is known to many as Belenus the Sun God. We take on different forms to our followers, as does the Court of Dark. Anyone worshipping a god or goddess of an element or nature is a follower of the Fae and under our protection. If you are unsure, you may ask Bishop Awynn. He will act as an advisor. There are plenty of other religions for you to purge from England, but my followers are not among them. They are not violent or harmful."

Mary returned to the rosary, rubbing each bead between her fingers. Her narrow lips moved fast again as she seemed to seek guidance from a higher power. "What tribute might I give on the solstice?"

Queen Aurora glanced down at the beads rolling between the human queen's slight fingers. The gold beads of the rosary caught the light as they glinted and shone in anticipation of her answer. Mary wanted reassurance Aurora's request would not cause her to act against her Catholic religion; this, Aurora understood, was the true root of her question and anxiety.

Aurora put her hand to her chest for a moment. She found the human queen's loyalty to her belief endearing. "You may leave a bouquet of lavender, lily, and rose out on your windowsill on the night of the summer solstice. On the night of the winter solstice, leave a combination of hawthorn, sandalwood, cedar, ash, and thistle as tribute to the Court of Dark. This is all I require as tribute, and I ask you to do this while you are with child. Just once."

Queen Mary inhaled, and her body relaxed under the weight of the tension she held. Her eyes were clear as she met Aurora's. "I shall have a child this way, I have your word?" she asked very carefully.

Aurora took Mary by the hand. "By my blood, you will have a child, Your Highness."

Without hesitation Queen Mary grabbed a dagger from her belt and cut her own finger. She held her index finger up for Aurora to see the crimson droplet swell and run down. "Then by mine own blood 'tis done." Aurora pointed to where Mary should place her blood signature. Mary signed the paper, and as she drew her finger away, the contract flew to Aurora.

"*As it is above, so it is below.*" Aurora spoke the words as the contract rolled itself up into a neat cylinder. She asked Mary to place her finger over hers, and Bishop Awynn placed his over both of theirs. His imprint sizzled for a moment as he spoke his oath over the rolled-up contract.

"I, Bishop Awynn, last of the Fire Drakes, bear witness to this Contract of Changeling between Queen Aurora of the Court of Light and Queen Mary of England and Ireland. It is sealed now and forever."

A blackened symbol appeared on the parchment. The contract glowed and levitated again, sparking before raining down in gold glitter.

Bishop Awynn handed a gold pouch to Queen Aurora, who presented the pouch to Mary. "Queen Mary, this gold pouch is to be used on your future husband the night you would like to conceive your child; stir this powder in with his dinner wine. He will not wake until morning."

The human monarch inspected the pouch, furrowing her brow. She opened the pouch to smell the powder. "'Twill not harm him?"

Aurora touched Mary's cheek with the back of her hand in a soft caress. "No, Your Grace, it will just help him to sleep through the night while your Fae friend visits you." Mary exhaled.

Bishop Awynn offered Aurora a silver pouch next. "You must begin taking this tea thirty days before your wedding night. Drink this every morning on an empty stomach. It will ensure you will conceive."

Queen Mary bowed. "I am most grateful."

Queen Aurora smiled. She sensed how much Mary wanted a child, but while she could help her conceive one, this would not make the human queen's soon-to-be husband love her the way she wanted him to. "Go now, Your Majesty, and be at peace. Know your request has been granted. You are a friend of the Fae." Queen Aurora kissed Queen Mary softly on each cheek and guided her to Bishop Awynn. Raising her palms together to her lips, she watched Queen Mary walk away.

Mary turned to give one final good-bye to the Fae queen. "I shall not forget your kindness."

Queen Aurora nodded, forcing a grin, her eyes narrowing on the monarch. As Queen Mary left, unease crept up her spine. *Yes, Queen Mary is well mannered, unlike her father. But Henry's blood still runs in her veins. It would be best not to forget she is still a Tudor*, Aurora chided herself.

Chapter Eight:
LOGISTICS

B ishop Awynn returned to the Court of Light to confer with Queen Aurora and the other bishops about the details of Queen Mary's contract. Entering the room, he found the atmosphere was not as jovial as he had hoped it would be. "Merry Meet, Queen Aurora." He noticed the thick tension in the room. "Merry Meet, Bishops." He glanced in their direction, seeking a hint to the problem.

"Merry Meet, Bishop Awynn. Did Queen Mary find her way home?"

"Yes, she did. She was most grateful, Your Majesty." He hoped it would alleviate her troubles.

Aurora stood and paced, her energy wings sprouting from her back, denoting her growing worry. The bishops said nothing and sat in contemplation. Aurora made the easy transition from walking to floating in a few strides.

Bishop Awynn was the first to rupture the stillness. "Your Grace, what causes you such turmoil?" He posed the question softly.

The queen did not break her stride, nor did she look at Awynn as she spoke. Aurora tapped her chin rhythmically as she floated. "Bishop Caer, Queen Mary will mate with Sir Arthur of the Dinay Mera clan, one of the last viable males of the clan. Therefore, I am well within my rights of the treaty. Make him aware of the arrangements. I am hoping Sir Arthur will be less likely to produce physical Fae attributes with a human. Their clan are freshwater elementals. The child may feel the call of Water or have a connection with it, nothing unusual. I gave Queen Mary explicit instructions for her tributes on both the winter and summer solstices during gestation, which satisfies the treaty."

"Yes, Your Grace. A shrewd choice for reproduction" was Bishop Caer's monotone response while he took notes.

"Bishop Awynn, to answer your question, I don't trust Queen Mary. I don't know why, but something from all my years of dealing with humans, especially her father, tells me not to trust her. Therefore, I am sending you to her court. You will keep watch over her. There is too much riding on this. In retrospect, I should have had Lady Sybella present, but it is too late now. I am bound by my word." Aurora tightened her mouth and balled her left fist, struggling to regain her composure. She squared her shoulders and shook her head, releasing her fist. "No matter. I see my misstep. She is but a human queen, and with you there to look after her, we will see she holds to her word."

"Why not have Lady Sybella read the contract now?" Awynn asked, shrugging.

Geddes huffed.

"Even if Lady Sybella reads the contract now, Mary might not have had any ill will at the time of signing it. I am still bound by my word. If she goes back on hers, we will deal with it then," Aurora replied.

Bishop Ward fixed his golden hair, smoothing it into a ponytail. "What is the human adage? Ah yes, you are borrowing trouble, Your Grace. Mary is not Henry."

Aurora glared at Ward. "Are you sure you want to dance with that particular dragon, Ward?"

Bishop Ward sank down in his chair.

Floating above her bishops, Aurora returned to her statuesque and regal posture as she floated. "I trust you, Awynn, to keep an eye on Mary."

"As it is above, so it is below," Bishop Awynn said, bowing.

"Go to Lady Sekhmet, who will be your contact on this. She will know when Mary is with child and when will be the right time for you to join her court. She will know when the pregnancy is viable."

Awynn exited to speak with Lady Sekhmet. The other bishops exchanged sideways glances, but nothing escaped Aurora's attention. Without turning her head, she spoke: "Bishop Geddes, speak your disapproval with my decision."

Bishop Geddes stopped stroking his goatee, stood, stepping forward to look up at his floating queen. He swallowed and glanced at his peers for support, but they offered him none. "I am concerned, given Bishop Awynn's inexperience in dealing with humans, Your Grace."

Queen Aurora floated down to face the remaining bishops. "I appreciate your concern, Bishop Geddes. However, Bishop Awynn has proven more than capable when dealing with his own followers, and he will not be alone. Yes, he is young, but he is still a bishop. You were all young and inexperienced at one point, and I allowed you to prove yourselves. While this is important, he needs to gain experience. You will all see that he succeeds, for if he does, then we all do. If he fails, then we all will. Am I clear?" Aurora glowered at the three bishops, pointing at each one.

They rose and bowed. "Yes, Your Grace," their voices sang out.

Chapter Nine:
A Fae in Queen Mary's Court
(circa late November 1554)

L ondon in late November was colder than usual as
winter took England into its fold. The dark night
held all her mystery; even silver moonlight could not pene-
trate the grey clouds streaking the navy sky. Bishop Awynn
arrived via Queen Mary's fireplace in his usual fashion.
Queen Mary was up late working on needlepoint. She sat
by the fire humming to herself in her muslin sleeping gown
and nightcap. Her shapeless attire hid the small protrusion
indicating her pregnancy. However, Lady Sekhmet—worshiped as Mother Nature—had a gift for detecting fertility
and conception.

Queen Mary was not startled by Bishop Awynn, as she
had advance notice of his arrival, but she was not pleased
to see him either.

"Bishop Awynn, to what do I owe this late-night intru-
sion?" Queen Mary said, glancing up between her stitches,
refusing to stand or curtsy.

Standing just outside the hearth, Bishop Awynn bowed. "Please forgive my visit, Your Highness. Queen Aurora sends her greetings. She has also sent me to watch over you during this delicate time of your pregnancy. You received her letter?" He smiled and kneeled in front of her to show he was amicable to all human customs.

Queen Mary picked up the pace of her needlepoint during his greeting, giving him a fleeting glance. Bishop Awynn cocked his head to the side. Gone was the desperate woman he had met a few months before.

Queen Mary set aside the blackwork needlepoint taught to her by her mother and strode over to him. The sleeping shift she wore could have been a brocade ballgown with the way she carried herself. Her chin held high, she narrowed her eyes. "Bishop, answer me. Thy queen does not trust me?" Her tone was of inquiry with a twist of accusation.

Awynn was almost impressed with her candor ... almost. "No, Your Majesty. Queen Aurora wishes you well. Any intelligent monarch makes sure her arrangements are beneficial for her people. A clever monarch will see it is fruitful for all parties involved. I am here to help facilitate."

Queen Mary bit the inside of her cheek but decided this battle was not hers to win tonight. "How do I introduce thee to the courtiers?" she inquired with an arched eyebrow. A yawn punctuated the end of her question, and she did not bother to stifle it.

Bishop Awynn gave a subtle smile. He had prepared for her questions. "I am a professor at Oxford University, here to advise and help bridge the gap between the old religious factions in Ireland and England."

Queen Mary shrugged halfheartedly at his quick response and turned away, pacing for a moment. "Most earls, barons, and dukes educate their sons at the university. They know the professors, and your language is not quite correct." Arms behind her, she shifted her weight from her heels to her toes, waiting.

"I have been on sabbatical in Wexford, Your Majesty, observing the druids; it will also explain my unique dialect." There was a gleam in Awynn's eye.

Queen Mary clucked her tongue and pursed her lips. "I can see why thou art one of Aurora's advisors. The lady hath chosen well," she said, looking him up and down.

"Thank you, Your Grace. *Queen* Aurora is a wise ruler on her own." He had noticed her slight.

"Very well, Bishop Awynn, and how shalt thou be addressed whilst thou art at court?"

"I am not a bishop of your religion, and I would be blasphemous by keeping the title while I am in court. What do you suggest, Your Highness?" Awynn bowed his head.

Queen Mary fixed her eyes upon the slender, white-haired man. *He is far too young to have hair as blond as starlight. It is otherworldly.* She had not noticed in their previous meetings how his hair was streaked with the finest silver. It glistened and reflected the fire like diamonds were hidden in each individual strand. Mary shook her head when she caught herself staring. "Why art thou called bishop, then? Is it not a religious title?

Awynn jerked his head back. "The title of bishop is one steeped in tradition. Without being pedantic, Your Highness, simply put, in Fae culture *bishop* means advisor. There is no religious significance." He was not about to divulge that the title was one of the few traditions Queen

Aurora had adopted from their old lineage as Angels. He was not lying; the word *bishop* did mean advisor, but it had come from the Shining Kingdom above.

Queen Mary studied Awynn. She was bothered by his presence. This felt controlling to her. She didn't like it one bit. She was the queen of her kingdom, not Aurora, but it was a means to an end. She rubbed her temples, contemplating the issue. Then she grinned knowingly. "Fine, I shall refer to thee as Viscount Awynn. I cannot give thee a higher title since thou holdst no land; it would be the cause of gossip if I did. Thou shalt stay in court. My lord chamberlain shall make the arrangements." She held her chin high.

Awynn bowed again. "You are most wise and gracious. Thank you, Your Majesty."

Queen Mary walked to her armoire and pulled out an ornate eggplant-colored, gold-brocaded robe. It had voluminous sleeves and a high collar and floated away from Queen Mary's body. Wearing it, she was demure and perfectly concealed. Queen Mary fixed herself in her mirror, and once she had decided she was presentable, motioned for Awynn to follow her to her sitting room. There she gestured for him to sit and glanced at the fireplace with its dying fire. Awynn took the hint. With a flick of his wrist, the kindling began to glow. Within a few moments, it was a roaring fire.

Bishop Awynn eyed Queen Mary as she smoothed her robe. *Perhaps Queen Aurora is on to something. Queen Mary's sense of entitlement is rearing its head like a snake in the garden after pruning. She has the Fae's cooperation; she could let her mask slip now. She has eased into her role as monarch, ordering those about her. Yes, Queen Mary is most definitely Henry's daughter, and Queen Aurora was wise to send me here to keep an eye on her.*

Queen Mary made herself comfortable on her bench, folding her legs underneath her. She rang the brass bell, and a few minutes later, an older gentleman shuffled in, still wiping the sleep from his eyes and coughing. Sir John Gage hobbled into Queen Mary's sitting room. Awynn gathered from his energy signature he was close to seventy-five years old. The man was unwell and had two years at most before his physical body expired. Bishop Awynn felt a pang of guilt for causing him to leave his bed this late. Queen Mary, on the other hand, felt no such shame, as was evident from the roll of her eyes.

"Sir John, so valorous of thee to join us," she said with a heavy sigh at his tardiness. "May I introduce thee to Viscount Awynn. He shall be my honored guest; see to his needs. Viscount Awynn, this is my lord chamberlain." She gestured with a limp wrist between the men.

Awynn stood and bowed. "'Tis a pleasure to meet thee, Sir John," he said, hoping he spoke in the correct tone. The Fae had quickly realized he had not paid much attention to the vernacular of the humans.

"Viscount Awynn, the pleasure is mine." Sir John turned his attention to the queen. "How long shall your guest be staying with us, Your Highness?" His voice was hoarse from sleep.

"Until Epiphany, Sir John. See the gent is made comfortable." Queen Mary gave the men a wave of her hand in dismissal, and the two bowed.

"Valorous night, Your Highness," Awynn said as he left the room. Sir John looked exhausted, and Awynn could not bring himself to ask the old man to escort him anywhere. Luckily, Awynn learned, everything in this court was delegated.

Sir John gestured for Awynn to follow, mumbling. They walked the hallway to a small alcove with two chairs flanking a large, elaborate tapestry. "Prithee, Viscount Awynn, I shall see to the quarters." Sir John waddled away without giving Awynn a chance to answer.

As Awynn took a seat, he noticed the exquisite crafts-manship of the chairs. The dark, polished wood reminded him of the amber wall in the Great Hall. He ran a delicate finger along the carvings on the back. There were flowers with filigree and ivy leaves melding into each other. He thought about the time and care it must have taken the artist to construct this piece. *Humans could be capable of so many wonderful things when they weren't consumed by lust or hate,* he thought.

As Awynn analyzed the tapestry, he heard the shuf-fling gait of Sir John's approach, only this time he was not alone. Accompanying him was a young woman with gold-en-brown hair peeking out from under a white cap. She had high cheekbones, full pink lips, and dark-brown eyes with flecks of gold. But she wore a look of exhaustion from a hard life of servitude. Awynn stood upon the girl's arrival.

"Viscount Awynn, this is Marjorie. The girl shall escort you to your quarters and see to your needs. I shall take my leave." Sir John abruptly hobbled away, eager to get back to his bedchamber.

"My lord." Marjorie curtsied and smiled.

Awynn bowed his head. "Marjorie, 'tis a lovely name," he said politely.

"This way, my lord."

Awynn nodded and followed her down the hallway. Queen Mary's palace was divine, the stained-glass windows bearing the royal crests glistening in the candlelight. The hallway candelabras cast a soft, warm glow, making the enormous drapes and the stone feel a bit less cavernous. He caught Marjorie staring at his hair as it twinkled in the candlelight. He pulled his hood up, scolding himself for not shifting his hair before entering Mary's chamber. *These are immature mistakes I cannot afford to make. No matter. I can play it off as the lighting and the late hour. I remembered everything but my hair, damn it to Lucifer.* Awynn knew the other bishops doubted his ability to handle this mission. He was determined to succeed, to not get caught up in the humans' problems or make silly mistakes.

Marjorie stopped at a door and wrung her fingers. As Awynn approached, her voice rose to a higher pitch. "Prithee, my lord, wait here, allow me to see that the room has been readied for you?" She pleaded with her eyes and repeatedly ran her hands over her apron, trying to smooth it.

Awynn understood her anxiety. Marjorie was afraid that if he was not satisfied with his accommodations, he might complain to the lord chamberlain. The punishment would then fall on Marjorie, when in all actuality, it was the lord chamberlain's responsibility to see that the room was ready. Sir John wanted to return to bed and most likely had not bothered to check if there were bed linens or a fire stoked in the room. Unfortunately, Marjorie would bear the brunt of Sir John's laziness and Queen Mary's lack of preparedness.

Awynn nodded and stood to the side, allowing Marjorie to enter his room first and take care of what she needed to. A few minutes passed before he overheard Marjorie preparing to start a fire.

Awynn entered the room. Marjorie was covered in soot, attempting to clean out the fireplace. "Oh, Marjorie, please, I cannot allow thee to." Awynn tried not to sound abrasive.

Marjorie gasped and jumped to her feet.

He helped her up and cleaned her off, but she recoiled from him, either from shock or an issue with class.

"I'm sorry. I like to make my own fires. It reminds me of home." Awynn smiled to ease the tension.

Marjorie exhaled, placing her hand to her chest in relief. "Forgive me, Viscount Awynn."

Awynn shook his head. "There is nothing to forgive. Thou hast done nothing wrong. The room is lovely."

Marjorie picked up the candelabra from the table and motioned for Awynn to follow her into the other room. «This is your privy chamber, and you saw the study. I shall wake you tomorrow morning,» she said as she grabbed extra linens from the armoire. «Valorous night, viscount.»

Chapter Ten:
WHAT'S IN A SOUL?

A urora took a breath and unrolled the parchment with care, trying to steady her hands. She had the drawing for a few days but couldn't bring herself to look until now. As the illustration came into view, she let out a gasp. Hogal had done a wonderful job. It captured everything Aurora had wanted. Serena's obvious beauty and the mischievous glint in her eyes just before she said something she knew you weren't going to like but needed to hear. The tendrils of her long, wavy hair cascaded down her back. He even managed to include a few haphazard shells caught in her mane, though nothing Serena ever did was by accident. The only thing the depiction missed was the way the sunlight played off her stunning rainbow tail. But Hogal had assured Aurora the statue itself would not miss this most important detail. He had measured the placement and promised the composite he used would give off an incandescent glow. He had consulted with Malascola to place quartz prisms along the base to project rainbows onto her for an extra dash of magic.

Yes, Aurora thought, *this was a fitting tribute to her best friend and the first Fae faction to fall in the war.*

The tears came fast, but she held them back, wiping at her face. She would approve the sketch and tell Hogal to begin work immediately. She had selected a site next to the lagoon; after all, it was called Serena's Bay. In the meantime, she would ensure peace reigned—Serena's death would not be in vain. Looking down at Serena's face drawn in exquisite detail, she thought about their last conversation, how apropos it was. How Aurora wished she could have had one more conversation with Serena! Aurora had taken it for granted and assumed there would be more, many more; but alas, there were not. She closed her eyes and held on to the sweet memory of their day: the salt scent in the air; the warmth of the sand under her feet; Serena making her usual dramatic entrance, undulating and riding the turquoise waves as she made her way to the beach. Her melodic voice.

"Well, look at you, Rory! Creating a new dimension, being the number-one goddess to the humans, and declaring war. What? You needed another challenge?" Serena teased.

Aurora splashed water at her friend. "What did you think of yesterday's meeting with all of the heads of houses?" She wanted an honest opinion, and Serena would deliver whether Aurora liked it or not; in fact, she was counting on it. Serena looked toward the water for a moment, collecting her thoughts. The wind whipped her blond, sun-streaked hair around her face. "You mean the part where you told them we were at war with a group of former Power Angels who rode dragons and were hell-bent on destroying us?"

Aurora clucked her tongue. "Um ... yes, Serena, that part."

Serena rolled onto her stomach and flapped her tail in the sand, making the annoying wet sound that Aurora hated. "Well ... you were diplomatic in your words, which was good. The Will-o-Wisps, did they really drop the from their kin name? I liked it better... Anyway, they are ready to fight, but they always are. The House of Hathor seems to be in your corner. The Fire Drakes pulled their passive crap, which I still don't get, considering their power. But you know Lady Kit, she will come around. She just loves playing the hero, which is going to get her in trouble one of these days. As for the rest, they seemed more scared. You will need to be strategic. Use Desdemona. No one knows these Power Angels—Dark Fae, or whatever they are calling themselves now—better than her." Serena's eyes focused on Aurora. She picked up a long, conical seashell and used it to emphasize her point as she spoke. "Use her, and don't let the idio—bishops, I said bishops—tell you otherwise."

Aurora looked at the seashell the Mermaid was pointing at her. She shook her head. "Did I make a mistake by not taking their offer? Am I serving us up to the dragons for a meal?"

Serena immediately sat up, plunging the shell like a dagger into the sand, shattering it. Her eyes turned red, emphasizing her anger. "Is that what has you all worked up? Look, Rory, I would rather die than be enslaved. King Varjok, whatever his name is, cannot be trusted. His offer was for us to live in fear. NO! You made the only choice! The right choice. We stand, and we fight! We might not be Power Angels, but we can fight."

"But can we? We have never seen war. We observed a war going on above us, but we chose not to involve ourselves. We don't know combat. Lucifer and his army never touched us.

He never even thought to engage us. Didn't you ever wonder why? I did. It's because we weren't a threat to him."

Serena shook her head, eyebrows knitting together. "Maybe you are correct—we were not a threat. We had the Power Brigade to fight our battles, and frankly, we were spoiled and pampered. We aren't anymore. I adore my life now. I love my faction. Back then, yeah, I thought I liked my life, but I didn't know any better, and damn it to Lucifer, I do now, and no one, not Lucifer or this Dark Fae king, is taking it away from me. So, I am ready to fight to my Oblivion."

"I guess that's the other part, Serena. Many will meet their Oblivion over this. My decisions directly affect the lives of my kin." Aurora knew her friend would figure out what was truly bothering her: guilt.

"Oh, Rory, you are frightened and already feeling guilty for things that haven't come to pass. Yes, Fae will meet their end in this war, but if they feel even a tenth of what I feel, believe me, it is better to go into Oblivion freely than live a life of unhappiness. In this realm as Fae, we have learned to love. We have factions and kin. We never had this as Virtues. We lived to serve, only knowing what we were told. As our queen, you have given us a sense of community and independence."

Aurora smiled at her friend's words. "It is why I want to protect it, but at the same time, I don't want Fae to cease to exist."

Serena reached for Aurora's hands, grasping them tightly to her heart. "You can't control everything, Rory. We live, we love—and if an Elestial Blade is our end, so be it."

Serena gave her trademark half-smile but had a glint in her eye, which meant there was a lesson coming next. Aurora braced for what was to follow.

"Rory, who says it ends at Oblivion?"

Aurora took back her hands. "We don't have souls. We die and we meet our Oblivion—"

"Who says we don't" Serena shook her head. "Who says Oblivion is it for us? When we were Virtues, we were told those rules. But we aren't Virtues anymore, and we haven't been for a very, very long time. What makes a soul? I can love. I can sing. I know right from wrong. When I see one of the sea creatures give birth, I get a pang deep in my heart because I wish very much I could. I have observed these humans and what they do to each other, and I question if they know right from wrong. Why do we accept they have souls and we do not? I have watched you care for all of them—all of the creatures on this planet. Surely you must have a soul. So, how do you define a soul?"

Aurora stood and paced, a clear sign the question had disturbed her. "I can't answer," she said quietly.

"Which part? Why they have souls or how to define one?" Serena looked up, chin resting on her hands.

"I guess a soul is energy. The immortal piece of the divine puzzle. Always looking forward to returning to the whole." Aurora glanced up at the sky. "Humans are in His likeness, and they have a piece of Him in them. Their souls have a spark of His light, and it wants to reunite with Him when their human body no longer contains it."

Serena smiled. "Therefore, by your definition, their body is a prison for their soul? And a soul is immortality realized? Then by your word, we Virtues were walking, talking souls. We were immortal. We may no longer be immortal, so perhaps we have a soul?" The glint had returned to her eye.

Aurora dropped to the sand, her shoulders rounded, her chin dipping to her chest. She lifted her head to look at the

Mermaid. "I think it is much more complicated, Serena."
Aurora's voice cracked; she didn't really have an answer.

"Well, if you ask me, I like to think a soul is a way back
home. If a soul is nothing more than energy and a piece of
Him, then as long as I have breath and a spark, it is in me to
do what I please. However, once it goes out, it is because He
calls it home, not because I cease to exist. So, I reject the idea
of Oblivion. Say what you want, but I think there is more to
all of this. I'm willing to fight for this life, and when it's time,
I will see for myself what comes next."

Aurora shook her head, chasing back the memories
and wanting to hold on to them at the same time. "Damn
it to Lucifer, Serena. I hope you were right and there is
something after this life. I miss you so much."

The Mermaid's words had haunted Aurora since their
conversation. It was strange, but since her passing, every
now and then, Aurora caught the scent of salt air when
she was alone at night. She swore that she heard Serena's
laughter in the waves. She had dismissed the sounds and
scents as longing for her friend, but maybe it was something more.

Chapter Eleven:
ASSIMILATE

Knock, knock!
Early morning came far too quickly for Awynn. The alkaline-and-lavender scented bed linens and the unfamiliar castle sounds had made for a fitful night's sleep.

"My lord," a woman whispered. Her knock became louder, more insistent.

Awynn recognized Marjorie's voice and rose to place a robe over the itchy muslin sleep shirt. He scratched and pulled at the uncomfortable material, which felt like sandpaper on his skin. The modesty humans needed in this era was not something he planned to get used to. It was also customary for humans to bathe in a linen shirt, which to him evaded all logic—the humans were prudish with their naked bodies, yet they bed-hopped like a Will-o-Wisp needed a reason to fight. *Go figure.* He buttoned his robe, catching a glimpse of his glowing hair and skin. He made sure to dim his glow as he answered the door.

Marjorie was bright-eyed despite this early hour. "Valorous morning, my lord."

He stood to the side to invite her in, but she did not move. She blushed. "I cannot come inside; would be in poor taste for me. Do you need help drawing a bath and dressing this morning?" She lowered her gaze, avoiding his eyes.

"But last night-" Awynn stopped, realizing Marjorie had helped because Sir John had delegated his responsibilities to her, and it being so late, the man was confident no one would have seen her. Besides, what was the reputation of a lowly chambermaid to Sir John anyway?

Awynn ran his hand over the back of his neck. "Coming off sabbatical, I did not make arrangements for my servants to meet me at court. I will speak with the queen about this, but perhaps you could help me this once?"

Her cheeks turned a soft shade of pink again, and she peeked down the hallway. Sir John had stationed Awynn in the private base area at Hampton Court.

"Aye."

Marjorie explained there would be many eyes on him, and she was aware of the rampant gossip among the very jealous courtiers. She waited until she was sure no one was around and then scurried into the room.

"I will help you, but the queen's permission is needed if this is to continue," she whispered.

Awynn smiled and kissed her hand in a chaste manner. "I thank thee, sweet Marjorie." He was not about to bathe in front of her with the linen shirt on, nor would he wait for the water to boil on the fireplace when he could warm it with a flick of his wrist. He had to draw the line somewhere. "Marjorie, I will bathe this evening. It helps to relax me."

The young woman stopped gathering the pails for water in his privy chamber. "Very well, my lord." She pulled the clothes Aurora had gifted him out of the armoire and laid them out.

"Marjorie, I have not yet been privileged to appear at Queen Mary's court. I have visited other monarchs, of course, but not hers. What is the daily routine here at the most charming Hampton Court Palace?" Awynn had to gather some information.

Marjorie went to remove his sleep shirt, but Awynn backed away. "Forgive me, my lord. I did not mean to offend you." She bowed.

"You did not, but I can remove my own dressings, please. You do not have to." Noticing the hurt in her eyes, he said, "I am sorry, Marjorie. Where I come from, we do not receive help in undressing."

She gave a half-smile in acknowledgment.

"It will take some time for me to get used to the customs, so please be patient with me. I have been on sabbatical studying for so long with the druids, where such formalities were not needed," Awynn added to soften his rejection.

Marjorie nodded in understanding, averting her eyes as he removed his sleep tunic. She handed him his underpinnings in the correct order. Awynn was grateful because he had no idea how to dress in proper human clothing. First, Marjorie passed him the nether hose for his lower legs, then the upper hose that covered from his thighs to his waist. His codpiece Awynn found most unusual; he squatted and danced about to get the piece to fit comfortably but found it was impossible. There was a high-necked doublet under a dark-brown jerkin and gown. Awynn's sleeves were made of silk strips and fastened with jewels, as was fashionable. He placed the ring his queen had given him upon his finger and donned his black velvet hat to complete the outfit. He felt ridiculous and was positive he looked the part as well. The shoes were tight, the hat was itchy, and all the ornaments made him feel like a jewelry box from Hogal's workshop.

He looked at Marjorie's plain grey dress and white pinafore. "Is that your uniform?"

"Aye."

"If you are to escort me and be my confidant, we will need to do something about it," he said with a smile, but she dropped her head.

"Nay, my lord, 'tis not allowed. I am not born with the right to wear such finery." She refused his gaze.

"Nonsense. You are helping me. Compensation is fair."

"'Tis not proper. I am in the queen's service. Thou wilt anger her." Marjorie folded her arms around herself, her chin dropping to her chest.

"I shall speak with her."

She protested, but Awynn put his finger to her lips. Her eyes watered.

"Where is Her Majesty?" he asked.

"Morning worship." Marjorie's voice cracked, and she swallowed. "Then the lady taketh a stroll in the gardens, but she will be surrounded by many courtiers. Oh, but the lady rideth later in the afternoon."

"Perfect! The queen would appreciate my company on her ride. In the meantime, may I have a tour of the gardens and perhaps some breakfast?"

Marjorie curtsied and led him toward the Great Watching Chamber, where Awynn was privileged to have his meals served unless the queen requested his presence.

She often dined alone but sometimes asked certain guests to sit with her.

"I shall go to the kitchen to acquire a bite of food, my lord."

Awynn nodded. "I thank thee." *I need to speak more in their dialect.* Many Fae had a knack for languages, but Awynn was not blessed with such gifts. Fire Drakes were not known for their linguistic skills, but rather, their innate charm. He had relied on that too much. However, between the *thee*s and *thou*s and the class rules of Mary's court, Awynn was finding he was more equipped to swim with the Water Kelpies of the River Ness at dinnertime than deal with these humans.

Awynn inquired of Marjorie what went on at court and the expectations of him as a guest. He did not understand the palace class system. He blamed his lack of familiarity on his time spent studying the druids and other pagan groups, and Marjorie did not question him. While he observed servants wearing distinctive colors somehow denoting their worth, he dared not ask Marjorie how she differed from them. For all the time he had spent around his humans, he did not understand them as well as he had thought.

Marjorie slipped into a hallway smelling of freshly baked bread. She pointed to a long corridor and told him to follow it, and she would meet him shortly. "Pray do not sit, my lord, until I return to wash you, and I'll find you a spoon as I did not see a utensil pack in your belongings."

Wait, did she say wash me? And what's this about a spoon? Awynn shook his head, mumbling aloud, "These humans and their noble customs confuse me more than a Fire-Breather needing a fire bellow."

He did as told and found himself in the Great Watching Chamber, a large dining room. The left side of the room became deathly quiet when he entered. Morning meal was almost over, but the women still lingered, gossiping.

Awynn felt every eye on him as he stood in the doorway.

Sir John was present and shuffled forward. "Valorous morning, viscount, 'tis a pleasure to see you. I desire you slept well?"

The man was much more amicable in the light of day. "Aye, I thank thee," Awynn answered as the ladies of court moved closer, inspecting him. He felt like he was surrounded by the Court of Dark's dragons as they readied for a feast. But he would rather have been with the dragons than these women. The dragons fought fair, and something told him these women did not.

Sure enough, the ladies converged on him, their chattering incessant.

"Is he married?" a courtier cooed, fanning herself and leaning forward until she was almost falling out of the top of her pale-green corset.

"How gained he such high favor with the queen?" Another in a deep-burgundy corset with long black lace double sleeves smiled at him and batted her eyes. She hip-bumped a third courtier out of the way, causing her to land on her seat.

How by all that is light in the universe do they know about me already?

Awynn reached for the poor girl, but her rigid corset sprang her upright, and she acted like nothing had happened. Another courtier pushed her way to the front of the group, making eyes at Awynn, while a courtier in blue looked like she was trying to unlace her competition's corset just to sit next to Awynn. They all asked questions as they vied for his attention. It was war here, and he was vague in his answers so as not to arouse too much attention or suspicion.

Marjorie came in with his food. Those who sat at his table had finished their second course, and the viscount was late. Marjorie had secured him a fresh-baked roll, cheese, and dried berries on a round silver plate. She presented Awynn with a small basin of rose-scented water, a linen cloth draped over her shoulder. Awynn stared at her as she nudged him with her eyes, glancing from the water, to his hands, and back again. The table's babbling grew still. Finally, the bishop swallowed and slowly dipped his hands in the basin, locking eyes with Marjorie for guidance. Her lips curved slightly as he took the linen and dried his hands.

Awynn thanked Marjorie as she placed his white napkin over his left shoulder and began serving him. The ladies scoffed at every move she made. They treated her in one of two ways: they either ignored her, or they went out of their way to order her around. Either scenario was not acceptable to Awynn. His blood boiled as the self-entitled women acted as if they were better than Marjorie because of chance, not hard work or accomplishment. Nothing about character or substance gave them their privileged existence. He observed Marjorie's lined hands and exhausted eyes while theirs showed no signs of fatigue. Why should they? The most tiring thing they had done all day was getting laced into their corsets.

"Sir John, I should like to ride with the queen this afternoon," Awynn said, thinking about how he could correct this injustice.

Sir John looked flabbergasted. "Her Majesty is occupied with matters of the kingdom. I am not sure 'tis possible, viscount." He stumbled over his words.

"Make it possible." Awynn pushed his plate away and smiled at the women. "It has been a pleasure, ladies.

"Come, Marjorie," he called and exited the dining hall to whispers. Marjorie was trying to clean up his plates, but he waved her to cease. Then, he discreetly placed a coin in the hand of a passing servant girl, whispering a thank you for her finishing up the job. The servant beamed at his generosity, but Awynn placed a finger to his lips and winked.

Once they were out of sight, he turned to Marjorie. "Go about your routine and meet me back at my room in the evening for dinner and to help me dress, please. I will speak with the queen this afternoon about making thee my groom if thou dost find this well?" He did not want to put any demands on her.

"Very much, my lord. I shall see your chambers are cleaned." She smiled.

"I thank thee."

She curtsied and took her leave.

Awynn watched her round the corner and returned to his room. He did not trust Sir John to deliver his message to Queen Mary. He blocked his door with the table so no one would walk in as he performed magick. Awynn started a fire with a flick of his wrist from the lit candles, causing the flame to jump into the hearth. Then, using a piece of parchment from his satchel, he wrote the queen a note requesting a ride with her this afternoon. He found the Chakra associated with Fire—the third one, located at the solar plexus—and envisioned the swirling golden-yellow vortex of energy.

"*Manipura*," he sang in the note of E. Literally translated, it meant "the shining jewel." In his mind's eye, he watched as the vortex became a lotus flower opening and a flame began to burn. "Thank you," he said, as the fire left the hearth and swam around him in ribbons of red, yellow, and orange. He held the parchment up for the ribbons of flames to take.

"*Let the flame burn bright, and let my words take flight. To Queen Mary let the smoke carry my message faster than a Pixie's wings. So mote it be,*" he intoned.

There was a flash of light, and the paper incinerated. The fire returned to the hearth, and he smiled; the queen would receive his invitation shortly.

On the other side of Hampton Court, away from the courtiers' gossip, Queen Mary reclined in her privy chamber, listening to her secretary give the daily briefings. She would begin hearing requests in a few minutes and was already bored.

Suddenly, she flushed. The fireplace roared, and her attendants all rushed to see what had caused the sparking. She clutched her rosary and felt a piece of parchment in her palm that had not been there a second ago. She knew what had caused the fire to roar out of control: her newest "courtier," Awynn. She unfolded the parchment and read his request. Mary was becoming more aggravated by her visitor. However, she was with child, and therefore she would tolerate him.

The queen cleared her throat to gather everyone's attention back to her. "I should like to ride with Viscount Awynn this afternoon. Bid Sir John see that my horses are made ready." She rolled her wrist instead of her eyes as she spoke.

The cool afternoon had a bite to it, reminding those residing in the English countryside that the official beginning of winter was a few weeks away. But Jack Frost did not bother with calendar dates. The winter tide arrived when he was ready.

The horses were restless in the stable, trying to keep warm. The stable boys worked overtime putting blankets on the animals and baling hay. Awynn waited there for the queen. Marjorie had secured him riding attire; how, he was not sure, and he had not questioned it. Even more reason to make his case to Mary for Marjorie to be his right hand for the remainder of his stay. Marjorie was proving trustworthy and resourceful, and he enjoyed her company. He could not help noticing the sadness swimming in her soul. He did not press her but hoped that one day she would share it with him, and he could help her.

The other bishops had often told Awynn he was too attached to his human worshippers, involving himself in their problems. Awynn did not share that perspective. If the humans were kind enough to put their faith in him and share their energy, he thought he should be willing to make their lives better. Awynn pondered all this as he stroked a black mare named Lady Jay. She nuzzled him and pressed her velvety nose into his hand.

"Would you allow me to ride you this afternoon, my lady?"

A nearby stable boy gave him a quizzical look for asking the horse's permission. Awynn smiled at him, but the boy ignored his genial gesture. To the stable hand, Awynn was just another spoiled aristocrat who could snap a command at any time, not a powerful and kind Fae.

My, how looks are deceiving.

The boy coughed and shivered in the cold stable as he tried to keep warm by moving about. He was only nine or ten, Awynn noted, judging by his inner light, but he looked older. *He has been through so much for a young human child.* The small fire in the stable was no more than a few dying embers. Awynn waited until the boy was at the far end of the stable, then with a quick centering of his energy and a flick of the wrist, the fire howled back to life, instantly warming the area around it.

When the boy returned, he was both thrilled and confused to see the roaring fire. He glanced around, then at Awynn, who shrugged, returning to stroking the black mare

Finally, the rustling of fabric let Awynn know Her Majesty approached. He offered her a low bow as was human custom. She did not have the entourage he expected, and relief washed over him.

"Your Majesty, you look lovely today." Awynn greeted her with a kiss on the hand.

"Thou art too kind," Queen Mary replied softly. "Didst thou choose a horse to ride?"

"Yes, I should like to ride Lady Jay."

Queen Mary strode over to the black horse with its white socks and pulled out an apple for the animal, feeding her as she stroked the horse's muscular neck. "Wise choice. She is a most magnificent mare."

She called out to the stable boy, "Fetch my horse."

"Yes, Your Majesty." The boy moved with swiftness, but he did not make eye contact with his queen. Keeping his head low, the boy grabbed the saddle and brushed a majestic chestnut steed. The reddish brown coat was shiny with a white blaze down its snout. The ebony mane was brushed and looked like silk.

Mary cut her eyes at Awynn. "Try to keep up, viscount." Her eyes twinkled as she mounted her chestnut horse side-saddle, and the boy led the horse out of the stables.

Awynn noticed the boy never garnered a second glance from the queen or a thank you. Her horse was well taken care of, better than the boy for that matter, yet she didn't acknowledge him, and the boy seemed to prefer it that way.

Curious.

Awynn followed, and they began a slow trot while making small talk. He looked behind and noticed no guards. Queen Mary took Awynn on the hunting trails and stuck to a slower pace until they were out of sight, where they came to a stop.

"Your Majesty? Is something wrong?"

Mary did not speak. She dismounted and removed her horned saddle, pulling out blankets from a hollowed-out log. She wrapped the saddle up in the blanket and hid it back in the log, something she had clearly done before. She remounted the horse, and he noticed the proper queen wore britches, much like his, under the plumes of her skirt.

The queen followed his gaze. "Bareback is the only way to ride, Viscount Awynn, but I am afraid ⊠tis considered plebian for a queen. I desire my secret is safe with thee?" She kicked her horse and galloped into the open field ahead.

"Of course, Your Majesty!" Awynn's smile grew. It was nice to see this playful side of Queen Mary. They rode for what seemed like the entire afternoon, the cool air whipping around his face as they raced along the English countryside. Mary was a good rider, and Awynn applauded her skills. Far from the castle, along a creek not yet frozen over, they finally gave the horses a much-needed rest and some apples.

The queen looked out over the landscape and breathed in the crisp air. "I am afraid this shall be our last ride. My physician has advised that riding in such a delicate condition is no longer conducive to my health. If thou wouldst meet later, come to my privy chamber in thy special manner once all have gone to sleep," she said, proving to the Fae bishop that she knew this was not just a casual ride.

"I thank you for your hospitality," Awynn said, before he asked her for his favor. "I have not seen your husband, King Philip. Is he well?" Awynn had heard the courtiers' gossip of the king's affairs in both England and Spain. They said the king showed affection for the queen but not love.

Mary's shoulders tightened, and her jaw clenched at the king's name. "The king's father did request the gent in Spain for trade negotiations. A queen needeth not a king. A queen can only count on her own power to rule. I am sure Aurora would concur." The queen's strawberry-blond hair peeked from under her cloth cap, frazzled from the wind. "Thou art most welcome here. Thy accommodations are to thy liking?" She smoothed her skirt.

"Yes, my room is lovely, and Marjorie has been very helpful, which brings me to my request. Since I am not familiar with the customs of your court, I would like Marjorie to be my escort during my time with you if you would be so gracious as to grant my appeal. She is knowledgeable and very loyal to you."

Awynn hoped that pointing out Marjorie's loyalty would make Mary more amenable to the request.

Mary pressed her lips into a thin line for a moment, her hands grazing her belly. Her gown hid the growing bump, and he worried she had overexerted herself with their ride. "Wherefore her?" She narrowed her eyes at him.

"Your Majesty, Marjorie is resourceful, and she is not indentured to any other courtiers. From what I have observed, all the courtiers have servants, yet I do not. To keep up appearances, I thought it would be best to have her pose as mine."

Mary stroked her horse's side. "Hast thou spoken to her about this?" She tilted her head.

"I have only asked if she would be interested in the position should you agree. Her response was that she would act if her queen wished it."

"Cunning wench," she mumbled, swallowing. Then Mary drew a loud breath. "I shall speak with her and inform thee of my decision this evening. Is that all?" The playful side of Queen Mary had seemingly disintegrated in the breeze.

Awynn gave Mary a side glance, not catching her insult. "This was a most enjoyable afternoon, Your Majesty."

She did not return the sentiment but turned to her horse as she spoke. "Let us return. I thank thee for the ride." She mounted her horse and in a flash, galloped back to retrieve her saddle and the trappings of the monarchy.

When Awynn returned from his ride to find Marjorie changing his bed linens, he informed her of the queen's words.

"Should I go to her?"

"Yes." Awynn watched Marjorie hurry down the hallway, then used the privacy to start a fire and write a letter to Queen Aurora. He updated her on what had transpired while he was at Hampton Court.

Something gnawed at the back of his head. As he penned the letter to Queen Aurora, his eye twitched. It was Queen Mary's insistence on meeting with Marjorie that bothered him. He believed there was more to it. Aurora's mistrust of Mary had taken root, and the reason why Aurora had insisted on his presence in *her* palace as the winter solstice approached was crystallizing.

Marjorie walked the lonely hallway toward the queen's privy chamber, her gaze shifting side to side as the candles cast a sickly glow on the walls. She clutched at her stomach, fidgeting with her apron. Staff bustled around her in their velvet uniforms, the line of demarcation between them. She was only afforded a plain white pinafore and grey tunic dress as a simple maid. When she arrived, the guards looked down their noses at her, but they opened the doors and allowed her to pass through.

Marjorie waited for Queen Mary in her sitting area. She knew better than to sit. She would stand until given permission to do otherwise. The queen's ladies-in-waiting said nothing to the lowly chambermaid. Marjorie tried to fix her bonnet, but compared to the brocade gowns of the ladies-in-waiting, Marjorie was as plain as the horse blankets in the stables, and in fact, those may have been prettier than her uniform.

A moment later, Her Majesty arrived. Marjorie gave a deep curtsy and waited until given her blessing to rise.

"Leave us," Queen Mary announced to the room, and the other women scattered like mice. Once they were alone, the queen extended her hand, offering Marjorie a seat. The young maid waited until the queen sat first, then took her place.

Queen Mary gave her a once-over, curling her lip slightly. "Viscount Awynn tells me he is pleased with thy services." The queen held up her hand, making sure Marjorie did not take the opportunity to speak. "That gent has asked me for permission to allow thee to act as his consort during his time here. I am willing to grant his request, but it is dependent on thee, my dear. As charming as the viscount may be, remember who thy queen is. When I ask thee for information on the viscount, thou shalt give it to me, Marjorie swallowed hard. "Aye, Your Majesty."

"Else I wouldn't be surprised to see the dogs thou art so fond of roasting over a fire."

Marjorie's face paled. The queen smiled. "Good. Tell Viscount Awynn his request is granted. Now go." The queen flitted her hand at Marjorie as if ridding herself of a buzzing insect.

Marjorie curtsied and excused herself, her heart pounding at the not-so-veiled threat. She wondered what the queen would ask of her. But if she was merely meant to report on the viscount, Marjorie decided, it wouldn't be so bad.

When Marjorie returned to Awynn's quarters with the news, he seemed glad to hear the queen had agreed to his request. "I will get you some clothes and speak with Sir John about a new chambermaid," he said.

But Marjorie insisted on continuing to clean his room. Deep down, she did not trust anyone else coming in, but she did not tell him. She explained it was in exchange for his kindness.

"I will need thee to accompany me to the events of the castle and inform me of protocol. It has been so long since I have been in court, I am afraid I am out of practice, my dear. I do not have friends here, and we both know how easy it is to offend." Awynn gave her a wink.

Marjorie smiled and nodded. "Aye, my lord."

"I am due to stay until Epiphany. Will that be all right with your family?" Awynn did not want to take her away from her obligations.

"I haven't much family. My father died two years ago, and my cousin is the baker; it is how I came to work in the castle."

"I am sorry," he said softly.

"It is not your fault he died. Wherefore are you sorry?" she asked, genuinely confused at his condolences.

"Because thou art alone. Thou art a good person, Marjorie, and thou hast suffered greatly. I feel for you."

Something in Marjorie clicked, and her hands balled into fists. She was not touched by his compassion but rather inflamed by it. "You do not know me. How can you say I am valorous or lacking valor? Do not take pity on me, viscount. I have done something to anger God, else I would have been born into better circumstances." Her cheeks flushed with emotion.

Awynn jerked his head back, stunned. "Because hard times have befallen thee, God is angry?" He scanned her face for a response. He had never heard this argument from a Christian follower, nor had he ever treated his pagan worshippers in this manner. *Is this what humans believe? When they go through bad times, their God is punishing them? Is this why the Court of Dark took such a stern hand with their followers? Are things so black and white for them?*

"Wherefore would God have chosen some to be rich and others to be poor? Some are kings while others are not," she said as if there was nothing Awynn could say to prove her wrong. But he resolved to show her with actions, not words.

Awynn gathered his thoughts, running his hands through his pale hair. "Marjorie, I cannot convince thee of thy God's intentions. However, I can try to show thee. I believe thou art a good person and God is not angry at thee. Sometimes life is just what it is, my dear. We each have our own light. We can either allow it to shine or let others dim it, but we choose to give others the power. No one takes it from us. No human or god has the right to dull thy shine. Material possessions, rich or poor—this does not determine one's brightness." He gave her an innocent kiss on the forehead and held her face softly between his palms. "A true god can see into one's heart, and any god looking into thine, Marjorie, would see how bright thy light is, and it is good. He—"

Or she.

"—would not sentence thee to a life of poverty. They would lift thee up. So do not blame God for the situation. If thou wouldst pray, then pray to be led to the opportunities to help thyself. The magick is within thee; believe in thyself."

Marjorie had stood frozen, listening to Awynn's words. On the one hand, they were blasphemous to all her religious teachings, but on the other, his words sang to a part of her heart that felt it true. Someone had finally spoken to her as a person and not as a lesser creature. She was grateful and a bit divided. Yet she perceived a shift deep down inside as if a tiny door had opened.

Chapter Twelve:
And So We Meet Again

P er the Treaty of Bodhicitta, King Jarvok needed to be made aware of reproductive arrangements with human monarchs. The treaty stated both courts shared equal tribute. The Court of Light acted as advisors in some way to most of the royal families of Europe, but the treaty specified they were not to influence the humans against the Court of Dark. Therefore, Queen Aurora must uphold her obligations to notify King Jarvok regarding her arrangement with Queen Mary. Following Fae protocol, the exchange of sensitive information happened on neutral territory, meaning emissaries from both sides met at the Archway of Apala.

Desdemona, captain of the Illuminasqua, did not trust anyone else to handle the matter; therefore, she acted as errand Fae for her queen. Normally the bishop who had arranged the deal was responsible for the meeting. But Bishop Awynn currently babysat Queen Mary, reporting back to Queen Aurora on her progress. Aurora had chosen now to deliver the details of the arrangement to Jarvok, based upon Awynn's latest briefing.

The other bishops should have taken action for their brother, but since when do they go out of their way to help anyone but themselves? Bishop Ward had a ready-made excuse claiming he was dealing with Indiga, his little niece. Yes, she was a handful, but Desdemona knew it was an excuse. Ward could care less about the Little One. She could have asked Nightshade, but having her second-in-command step in for her did not sit well with the proud warrior Fae. Besides, in a few Troll's blinks, she would be on her way home.

Desdemona used the journey as a training exercise, jumping and hurdling over fallen tree trunks like an obstacle course. When she reached the River Nimbue, she practiced her Water elemental defenses, creating little waves as she passed by—anything to sharpen her skills. Desdemona found a means to turn even the most mundane task into a worthwhile one.

Pausing upon the Bridge of Oroki, she paid her respects by placing a small piece of jeremejevite crystal at the bridge entrance. The periwinkle-hued crystal was small, only half the size of her index finger, with a triangular point slanted to the left. Jeremejevite was one of the rarest crystals on the planet. Desdemona had found a small reserve when she first came to Earth.

She admired the light-blue color, but the vibration spoke to her on a much deeper level. Aurora had explained the crystal could assist with adjustments, allowing the Fae who worked with the crystal to not only survive but thrive with change. Considering the transformations Desdemona had endured when she first came to Earth, it was no wonder the crystal resonated with her. The more she worked with it, the more the crystal helped with the grief and loss.

Whenever the captain came to the bridge, she brought a piece to help with the sorrow of the Fae lives lost during the War. She knew the cost of war all too well. Desdemona was a warrior at heart, hardened by the scars of battle. The factions lost in the war met their Oblivion because humanity no longer worshiped them, fading away when they were not needed. The Merfolk Faction helmed by Lady Serena came to mind, and Lady Lolita of the Abada Faction would never grace the Earth again. She bowed her head, touching her lips with three fingers, a Power Angel sign of mourning. She glanced side to side, embarrassed by the long-ingrained habit.

Desdemona despised that the Fae needed neutral territory. She hoped one day they would not, but as long as Jarvok held power, she felt her hope was a Little One's dream. She did not trust or like the king of the Dark Fae, and the feeling was mutual. The two had a history. They had squared off after she exalted. She could not remember what the argument had been about. She only recalled Commander Gabriel separating them after she cut Jarvok's face with her blade. Her lips quirked with her fond remembrance of Jarvok's blue blood welling to the surface and how his amber eyes had bulged when he realized she had cut him. *One day I'll finish what I started.*

Crossing the bridge, practicing her sword patterns, she carefully stepped, thrusting and parrying until a familiar hum of power hit her. Her skin prickled with energy, and she closed her eyes as she let it wash over her. Even though she was exalted, she could still sense another Power Brigade member; her Elestial Blade itched below her skin, begging to be unleashed. Her strides smoothed.

The aquamarine archway glittered into focus. A large white dragon stood waiting for her. Its black tail swayed back and forth like a cat toying with a mouse.

"Well, of course, he brought his best accessory," she mumbled.

Zion, Jarvok's second-in-command, leaned on Raycor's side, his arms folded and his ankles crossed. He pushed off the dragon with his elbows and sauntered toward the crystal-blue three-sectional arch, removing his Black Kyanite helmet and shaking out his shoulder-length blue-black hair.

Desdemona did not adjust her speed. As far as she was concerned, he could wait. She pulled the scroll out from her vest as she approached the middle archway and prepared to hand it off to him. Zion smirked and gave the traditional Power Angel greeting, placing his right index finger and middle finger to his forehead.

"Here." Scowling, she punched the scroll through the archway.

"What? No greeting for an old friend? Hi, how are you, Zion. My, you look well. What manners do they teach you in the Court of Light?"

"I do not have time for your games. Take the scroll to your king and be on your way." Desdemona pointed toward the way he had come.

"Tut, tut... not so fast. I have my orders to read the scroll upon receipt to make sure the contents are not, um, how shall I put this ... of dubious nature." Zion unraveled the parchment.

"Do you think I would haul my ass all the way out here to trick your king? Please." She rolled her eyes.

"Well..." Zion clucked his tongue. "While it is a fine ass to haul, my king does not trust you or your queen, so in a word ... yes."

Desdemona growled under her breath, and Raycor growled back, her neck muscles rippling as the sound echoed. Zion arched an eyebrow at his dragon's response. Without looking up from the parchment, he said dryly, "If it is a growling contest you would like, my dear, I can assure you, Raycor is up for the challenge."

With a lilt, Desdemona responded, "I've always wanted a pair of dragonskin boots." But she had pushed too far.

Zion crumpled the parchment and stuffed it in his hip holster. "Do not threaten my kin, Light Fae, or else I shall be the one wearing new boots made of your hide!" He tried to draw his blade, flicking his wrist, but nothing happened. He looked at his inner forearm, frowning at its lack of a weapon.

The archway's aquamarine stones slowly glowed, the blue rays blocking his blade from being drawn in anger and malicious intent.

"Bring it!" Desdemona said, not noticing the stones' shine.

"I do not need a blade to best you!" Zion snarled. Raycor roared, cheering him on.

A thundering came from above, interrupting the bickering Fae. Blue light emanated from the archway stones, bathing the two Fae and Raycor in its glow. They froze as voices ricocheted from the light. Desdemona and Zion went on the defensive, gazing upward to find the source, but the light from the stones blinded them.

"Enough! We as the Oracles declare the archway is under our protection. We will not have blood spilled on neutral ground. You are here to exchange the scroll. Do so now! You have been warned." The light faded.

Zion cast his eyes downward. Raycor dropped her long, sinuous neck, bowing her head and pinning her ears back.

Desdemona bit her lip as she lifted her hands in surrender. "Read the scroll so we can leave." Her voice hovered just above a whisper.

Zion nodded. He tried to smooth out the parchment as if erasing the wrinkles in the paper would undo their lack of self-control. His gaze passed over the words, and then he rolled it up, tucked it away, and cleared his throat. "I will deliver it to King Jarvok." He turned to mount Raycor, glancing up at the sky suspiciously.

"I did not know the Oracles could do that," he whispered to his dragon, who huffed in surprised agreement. Raycor checked the atmosphere, flicking her forked tongue. She ran in the direction of the falls, jumping in order to catch a current of air.

Desdemona watched Zion and the dragon leave, then followed suit. But two sets of eyes chased each Fae in their respective directions. A white bushy tail trailed behind Desdemona, and a long black body undulated under Raycor's shadow back to Blood Haven.

As the wind whipped around his head, Zion and Raycor exchanged a glance. They did not speak of it. Zion prayed to the universe that Lady Zarya would not tell his king about his lapse in discipline. He exhaled as he passed over the gates and did not see Jarvok waiting for him. If his king knew what had occurred at the archway, the delivery of the scroll would have happened in the combat circle, with Zion flat on his back after an ass-kicking. Instead, Jarvok waited for him in the strategy room, hands behind his back, staring out at the training exercises below. He was the epitome of quiet calm.

"You have the scroll?" Jarvok asked without looking at Zion.

"Yes, my liege."

Zion endeavored to read his king's expression. He knew what the scroll said, but he did not take for granted how Jarvok would interpret the situation.

"Queen Aurora evidently has some trust issues with the human monarch," Jarvok mumbled.

"In what way, my liege?"

Jarvok gestured with his finger for Zion to come closer. He spread the scroll on the table and pointed to the tribute section of their agreement. "Here she asks the monarch to leave tribute to our court first on the winter solstice."

Zion shrugged, still not making a connection. Jarvok stared at him. "If she trusted the human, she would have timed it differently. The human is indebted to the Court of Light, not us. This is testing the monarch by making her leave tribute for us first. I believe Aurora knows she may fail. If she does, Aurora can terminate the pregnancy immediately, and there is technically no harm to either side. She has not violated the contract. Now if the human monarch does not leave tribute for us and stays with child for even a second after her disrespect, I will waste no time taking action."

Zion rubbed his cheek with the back of his hand. "But wouldn't Aurora's Oracle have directed her on these issues?"

Jarvok clapped him on the shoulder. "You are thinking like a ruler; there is a way to check. Lady Zarya can let us know if the Court of Light's Oracle had any input on this contract. She could not read the human's intention because we did not draw it, but let's see if Aurora is as clever as she thinks she is. I do not believe her Oracle was present for this. The wording is off, and her Fire Bishop has taken up residence in the human monarch's palace. There would be no need if the Oracle had been there. Aurora is second-guessing herself." Jarvok took a piece of parchment, wrote a note, and whistled for Los. The small amber-and-black dragon flew into the throne room. He was never far from Jarvok. "Los, go to Lady Zarya. Deliver this note and escort her back to Blood Haven. She will be in meditation in the Polaris Hills."

Zion swallowed, thinking he had celebrated too quickly. Lady Zarya had been in meditation, which could be why she hadn't tattled on him. He could only hope that after her meditation she would be far too centered to dwell on his slight indiscretion.

Chapter Thirteen:
A Most Wondrous Time of Year
(December 1554)

As Christmas drew near, Hampton Court Palace buzzed with preparations. The staff worked tirelessly bringing in wreaths and evergreens. They swathed every buttress and railing in shades of green, red, and white. The scent of the forest drifted through the castle. During Henry's reign, the staff had not been allowed to decorate until Christmas Eve as it was considered bad luck, but Mary did not abide by such antiquated rules. The crisp mountain air permeated the stone walls, and for the first time in weeks, Awynn felt more settled, surrounded by such lush greenery. Each day, he looked forward to what new holiday delights the staff dressed the palace with. Boughs of holly hung over arches and doorways. White taper candles adorned the stained-glass windows, giving the castle an ethereal glow reminiscent of the Court of Light. He chuckled when he overheard a few servants refer to the candles as "fairy lights." Awynn was pleased watching these human traditions, though was unclear on how this translated into their Christian faith. As far as he knew, the holiday celebrated the birth of their Savior. How evergreens and candles represented this, he was not sure, but it was pretty to look at. Most of these traditions were born from the pagan faith, but he certainly would not tell them.

Most of all, Awynn was enjoying his time with Marjorie. She had opened up to him, becoming more inquisitive about his philosophy on religion. She admitted the pagan ways intrigued her. She had been educated to believe paganism meant eternal damnation. *To steer her away from biblical teachings and rework all she knew, everything her society was built on, might be asking too much of her,* Awynn thought. He avoided questions regarding his own beliefs; he was not here to convert her. Marjorie did want to learn more of the healers, and Awynn taught her about herbs, flowers, and their healing properties. She had an agile mind and a knack for the healing arts.

Every few days, Queen Mary summoned Marjorie to her side. When the young chambermaid returned, her light had dimmed. He knew Mary had questioned her, but he dared not ask. He wondered if Marjorie's light dimmed from lying to Mary or from telling on him. However, there was nothing to tell. Marjorie could report to Mary about the pagan teachings, but Aurora had a deal with Mary to leave the pagans alone. Of course, it did not mean Mary would want him preaching the ways of the old faith in her own home.

His shoulders slumped as he rubbed his temples. Soon none of this would matter, as the winter solstice was upon them. Mary would leave tribute for the Court of Dark, and

Awynn would stay a short time longer to determine if the child held Fae physical attributes in accordance with the contract. During the summer solstice, he would visit Mary again, ensuring she fulfilled her obligations.

Awynn glanced out the frost-covered window to remind himself to stay in the present. Today, he would gather the berries and plants needed for Mary's tribute. Marjorie would accompany him, and he would use their time to teach her about winter berries and the solstice.

A soft rustling of fabric and shuffling of feet paused his rambling mind. Awynn turned from the cold window as Marjorie cleared her throat. Dressed in a plain velvet gown of red, she appeared anything but simple. She smoothed the deep-red velvet with its cream loop embroidery and prattled on about feeling odd dressed in a gown just to walk outside.

Marjorie complained about these heavier gowns. With her standard uniform, she just had to contend with a chemise and a petticoat, but she explained it had taken six extra steps to get ready today. The false sleeves were especially puzzling to her; her brows knitted together as she pulled at the delicate lace. Awynn draped a cream-colored fur cloak over her shoulders and stepped back to admire her, raising his clasped hands to his lips. The ensemble was lovely on her. Her braided chestnut hair was tucked under the rabbit fur hat. She blushed, the color on her cheeks matching the gown.

She had caught the eye of more than one of the men in court, but she stayed by Awynn's side, never giving them a second glance. If Awynn had not spent so much time around the courtiers, he would have been happy for her and thought it a wonderful opportunity. However, he had discovered life at court was nothing more than a gossip mill. The women looked to cut each other down in their attempts to marry, the men were never faithful, and disease was rampant. He knew once he was gone, Marjorie would be treated poorly again.

Awynn saw the men act one way in front of each other, all chaste and proper, but behind closed doors they slept with their friends' wives and raised their hands to their women. The women were no better. They tried to seduce any man who looked in their direction, regardless of marital status or friendships. No, this was not the life for Marjorie, Awynn decided. He wanted better for her.

"Viscount Awynn? Are you well?"

"I am. You look exquisite. Shall we?" He smiled and gave her his arm.

They headed out of his room and down the corridor toward the gardens. They walked through the stark snow as the castle dogs Marjorie cared for frolicked and jumped around them. Marjorie threw snowballs at the beagles. Queen Mary had her cocker spaniels for hunting, but the beagles were left over from Mary's father, King Henry. The animal caretaker had continued to breed the beagles all these years. Eventually, when Mary took the throne, the remaining pups were relegated to the kitchen. Marjorie had taken a liking to them. Awynn found it sweet she had bonded with the abandoned animals. Her light grew stronger and brighter around them.

Every human had a light, and all the Fae could see it. The humans' light told a Fae their life expectancy. It was the soul's essence, the core of what made humans, well ... human. Some Fae saw colors in the aura and were able to distinguish a human's emotions. Awynn was not one of those. But Marjorie's was bright. She had taught him so much in the past few weeks, and he wanted to return the favor somehow.

Realizing she might have been inadvertently ignoring the viscount, Marjorie stopped playing with the floppy-eared dogs. Brushing the snow from her skirt, she stood. "What are we looking for on this day, my lord?"

He smiled at her change in demeanor. "We will look for items to make a tea, and I will teach you how the winter affects our hearts," Awynn said, inspecting the nearby plants and bushes. "Chilly weather can be hard on our hearts. The blood becomes more viscous, increasing the pressure. We can use herbs to lower the amount of work for the heart. Drinking hawthorn tea with cinnamon and rose petals helps. The berries and leaves of the hawthorn plant improve circulation. The rose petals act as to calm the nerves, and the cinnamon is for inflammation."

Marjorie's brow furrowed and relaxed, matching the cadence of his speech. She hung on to his every word. If he touched a plant, she did too, trying to mimic his touch and pressure.

Awynn found the ingredients, showing her what to look for in the berries. The color gave only a small insight into their ripeness, but a slight pinch told the true story. He rolled the berries between his index finger and thumb, illustrating how the skin peeled from the body of the fruit, noting the juice bursting from underneath the skin. The blush of the cold air colored Marjorie's cheeks with a soft-pink glow. Her chestnut eyes focused in contemplation as he explained the details.

They took the afternoon exploring the woods and collected the cedar, ash, and thistle he needed. It was almost dark by the time they returned to the castle.

"How about we eat in the room this evening, and I will show thee how to prepare the berries for the tea?" Awynn asked.

"Aye, I would enjoy it, my lord." Her eyes were bright. "I shall ask my cousin for some bread and dried fruit. 'Tis late, but she will help me." Marjorie hurried down the hallway.

Awynn started a fire and placed their day's work on the table. He would prep the tribute and deliver it to Queen Mary tomorrow.

Marjorie returned just as the sky darkened and candle glow was all that was left to light the room. The fresh-baked bread was surrounded by assorted dried fruit and walnuts, and she had brought a vessel of wine from the kitchen, all cradled in the crook of her arm. They ate and talked while he showed her how to dry the hawthorn berries properly and explained the significance of the thistle, cedar, and ash for the winter solstice.

He had also been teaching Marjorie to read. Awynn was well aware only girls and women in positions of wealth could even think of having access to resources for learning reading, writing, and arithmetic. Marjorie had proved an apt student. She was already through the simpler reading lessons and could write her name. He would arrange for a tutor after his departure to continue her studies. Perhaps he would even pay for her to go to school somewhere far from this life of servitude.

Awynn's prolonged stay among the humans had made him aware of the struggles they endured. He had prided himself on being in touch with his worshippers, more so than many of his kin. However, the time spent with Marjorie, listening to her stories and seeing her day-to-day life, had opened his eyes to what he had been doing wrong all this time.

Awynn was a visitor. He appeared to his humans for brief moments, took their accolades, saw them at their best, and vanished. Sometimes he saw them grieving for loved ones, stripped down to their raw emotions, but even then, it was just a glimpse. In his various incarnations, he had learned nothing of his worshippers. The humans gave him energy and time, and while he gave them attention, how could he say he gave them love when he knew nothing of them? He identified his high priests and priestesses by name and face, but not much more, not like he knew Marjorie. *Why couldn't I have taken the time to speak with them? Break bread with them? Would it have made me less of a god to do so? Could I not have walked among them as I have with Marjorie? Maybe make a real change.* He wondered whether the leaders of his groups were as petty as the courtiers here. That went against everything the Fae stood for. *Is my ignorance perpetuating it?* These questions needed his queen's attention.

Awynn glanced up at Marjorie as she hung the berries by twine. His heart warmed. He would be eternally grateful for her. He thought about revealing his true nature but worried it would complicate her life. Awynn shook his head as the answer floated in his mind. *It is best to leave well enough alone and reward her in the system and culture she is accustomed to.* A plan formed.

Marjorie finished with the berries and put a few stems in water to preserve their fullness just like Awynn had instructed her to do. She picked up her grey uniform and white pinafore, stepping toward the bedchamber as she did every night.

Awynn helped her change—in a modest way, of course—loosening the closures when she needed him to. But Marjorie had become an expert in removing complicated gowns and accoutrements, and she excused herself to finish the job. When she returned to their multipurpose area, gone was the velvet-clad lady from the day; the young girl of sixteen had reemerged. She wore the usual drab uniform of the lowly chambermaid, exhaustion settling upon her shoulders and her glow dimming with each step.

"I shall take my leave. Valorous night, Viscount Awynn." She curtsied, and he bowed back.

"I thank thee for a glorious day." Awynn walked her to the door.

As much as Awynn wanted to ponder the day and the philosophical conundrums of being a god, he had business to attend to on behalf of his own queen. He shimmered, his Fae skin and hair released in all their glory. The blond human tresses were replaced with his silver strands, kissed by the stars. His luminescent Fae skin sparkled in the moonlight. Awynn stood to his full height, pulled his shoulders back, and gathered the berries, cedar, ash, and thistle in a wooden bowl. He lit white sage, waving the bundle over the berries to allow the smoke to envelop the bowl, smudging the concoction of natural items, clearing them of any leftover signatures left by Marjorie. He tapped into his Chakras, starting with his solar plexus, which held his elemental connection. He allowed the power to flow until the rainbow column lit up, one by one: red, orange, yellow, green, blue, indigo, violet, and a bright white light from his third eye. The white light enveloped his entire body as he chanted:

"Mine is the magick; mine is the power;
Now is the time; this is the hour
I remember my light; I call to it make bright
Charge this offering; let it be right."

The spectrum of colors spread from his chest to his heart, merging into white light, traveling down his arms, out his hands and bathing the bowl in a glow. Taking a sharp inhale, he fell forward, exhausted, as the light dissipated. "It is done. Marjorie *is* a natural healer. Her signature was strong today. That took more energy to clear. He smiled knowing he brought her some joy. Their time spent outside with the dogs and learning spoke to her soul. This confirmed his plans for Marjorie.

"All Mary would have to do was leave it on her windowsill the following night for the Court of Dark.

Later, Awynn arrived in Queen Mary's chambers via his usual way, through her fireplace. She sat working on needlepoint again. He bowed, and she nodded in return, not bothering to stand. She pointed to her belly as her excuse, but he knew even if she were not with child, she would not move.

"Good eve, Your Majesty," he said.

"Valorous evening, Viscount Awynn." She did not glance up from her needlepoint.

"How are you feeling?"

She huffed. "As well as can be in my state."

Awynn tried to keep his temper in check at her lack of manners. In all honesty, Mary was just over five months, but acting as though she were due any day. "Tomorrow is the winter solstice. As per your agreement with Queen Aurora, you are to leave tribute for the Court of Dark."

She paused her needlepoint. "I am aware of mine arrangement, Awynn."

He wet his lips as the pulse in his forehead thumped harder against his skin. "I am sure you are. I have brought your tribute, which has been prepared to the specifications of the Court of Dark. All you have to do is place it on your west-facing windowsill after the moon rises but before midnight. Failure to do so will nullify your contract, and, well..." Awynn waved his hand in the air. "You will not forget, so there is no reason for us to discuss the ramifications of such a careless mistake. As a queen, you understand this would force my queen to act." Awynn's beseeching stare implored her to take the directions seriously.

"Art thou threatening me?" Her tone was so cold that icicles could have formed on her tongue. Her eyes narrowed.

Awynn raised his chin. "I am simply reminding you, Your Majesty. You have a contract with the queen of the Court of Light, so do not be flippant. Put your damn needlepoint down and listen to me!" His eyes ignited, their placid copper darkening like thunderclouds, crackling along with his rising temper.

Mary stood and threw her project to the ground. "How dare thee! I am the queen of England. Do not order me!" Pink dots appeared on her fair cheeks, and a large vein pulsated in her temple, matching the one thrumming in his.

Awynn did not want to concede, but he was a guest in her kingdom, and she was in a delicate condition. Diplomacy had to prevail. "I apologize, Your Majesty. I am concerned for you and your child. I was afraid you were not listening to my directions, and I know how hard it was to ask for help in conceiving this gift. I would not want to see you jeopardize your happiness over details. That is all," Awynn said with a bow.

Queen Mary ran a hand over her belly. "Perhaps we both did act out. I shall leave tribute. Valorous night." She took the bowl, the berries swirling up the sides with her quick gesture. She turned to enter her bedchamber.

Awynn left in the same manner in which he had come, but his mood had undergone a definite change.

Mary sat in bed, arms folded, grinding her teeth. The velvet canopy curtains of her bed were pulled back, allowing for an unfettered view of the fire. She gazed unblinking into the dancing blaze. The flames seemed to be taunting, challenging her, as though they were Awynn's minions, watching and laughing. *I allowed him to order me around in mine own domain, like a commoner.* Her nostrils flared. As the queen of England, she needn't bow to anyone, least of all a creature who practiced witchcraft. Only a week earlier she had received a copy of the *Malleus Maleficarum*, known as *Hammer of Witches* guidebook, and it was a Godsend. She was positive that if her father had possessed it, he might have saved himself from heartache. After reading it, she was all the more convinced that Anne Boleyn had made a pact with the Devil. The book stated that the practice of witchcraft was a criminal act against God. Heinrich Kramer had written the manuscript to help show the Devil came in many forms. *How could I have been so foolish? I made a mistake by bargaining with*

Aurora, a whore of Satan. Offering her a child, only to steal both our souls! No, I cannot allow it. I will not! Kramer said it all started with an innocuous task, something effortless. Eve took one bite of a simple apple. The bowl of berries, Mary thought, represented her apple. It was test, and she would not fail! She would not go against her Lord and Savior over a bowl of berries. As soon as her child came into the world, she planned to baptize the baby for protection. His grace would come upon Hampton Court once the demon Awynn left.

As for Marjorie, Mary could shave the girl's head and look for the mark of the Devil as the book stated, but Mary did not need confirmation; she was certain that Marjorie was in league with the Devil. She would not allow such a travesty in her kingdom. The girl would hang. *How dare these creatures come to mine own palace and tempt my subjects!*

Mary's eyes narrowed as she stared into the fire. She was determined her soul would not burn. *My God and faith are stronger than these demons and their witchcraft.* She began to recite her favorite prayer; since becoming queen she equated it to herself: "Hail, holy queen, mother of mercy! Our life, our sweetness and our hope! To thee do we cry, poor, banished children of Eve. To thee do we send up our sighs, mourning and weeping in this valley of tears. Turn, then, most gracious advocate, thine eyes of mercy toward us; and after this our exile show unto us the blessed fruit of thy womb." Mary touched her belly. A plan took shape to rid herself of her enemies. Her mumbling lips twisted into a sneer.

Chapter Fourteen:
DRAGON SITTER

K ing Jarvok called for Los and Zion. The two entered
the throne room ready to serve their king in any way
he commanded.

"My liege," Zion said with a bow. Los mimicked him
with a nod and folded his wings, his tongue lolling out of
the side of his mouth.

"Today is the winter solstice, and while I know your
covens and groups are set to leave tribute and worship you,
I need you to escort Los through the Veil to see if Queen
Mary made good on her word to Aurora."

Zion glanced at the small dragon and back at his king.
The winter solstice was a very important night for his followers. He was due to appear with Raycor at several covens
wearing his many Celtic god personas. Norse and Slavic
pantheons were also his territories. To have to dragon-sit
Los was not conducive to his plans.

Jarvok must have sensed the conflict in Zion. "I am just
as busy as you are on this most sacred day, Zion, but should
the human monarch not fulfill her obligations, this could

have dire consequences for our court. Aurora failed in her duties when she did not have her Oracle review the contract with the human, though whether this was an oversight or her ego, I am not sure. For that reason, I am not *asking* you to take Los, I am *telling* you to take Los through the Veil to observe the situation. I have read the contract; Queen Mary must leave tribute by midnight. If she does not, she is in violation. You will retrieve Los at midnight. You are free to see to your worshippers as he waits. Are we clear?"

"Crystal clear, my liege."

Jarvok faced Los. "You will monitor the human monarch, Queen Mary. She is to leave tribute for the Court of Dark on her windowsill facing the west. The energy signature will be the Fire Drake bishop from the Court of Light. Stay hidden and be safe, Los. You know how the humans will view a small-winged creature such as yourself. They are religious fanatics."

Los flapped his wings, lifting his head high and giving a small chortle in agreement.

"You will both leave at dusk," Jarvok commanded, dismissing them with a wave.

Zion cleared his throat. "My liege, if the human does not leave tribute, what are you prepared to do?"

Jarvok tilted his chin up, letting his white hair fall back; he brought a finger to the scar on his forehead and tapped it for a second before letting out a long, deliberate exhale. "If the human monarch's pregnancy is terminated immediately, I have no quibble; if not, I will pay Queen Aurora a visit at the Court of Light to remind her of our treaty and find out exactly why she would allow the human to disrespect my kin. Her answer will determine my reaction,"

Jarvok said flatly, his hands behind his back, a signal for Zion not to push him.

"Very well, my liege."

Chapter Fifteen:
LIKE FATHER, LIKE DAUGHTER
(DECEMBER 21, 1554)

Queen Mary sent for Marjorie after dinner. The monarch had been uncomfortable all day, stretching her back, placing her left hand on the arch and pressing on it as she groaned. She complained to anyone who would listen that she wanted to rest. The idea of dealing with the chambermaid was beneath her, but she pinched the bridge of her nose and dismissed her ladies after they prepared her for bed.

The bowl of berries stared at her like a yowling cat scratching to get in the house. The trunk that the errand boy had brought in from the stables still smelled of hay and horses, but it was a means to an end. She kicked it with her slippered foot in disgust as she drummed her fingernails on the bench, waiting for the girl. A quiet knock on the door startled her out of her roiling anger as her privy guard announced Marjorie's arrival.

"Come." Queen Mary's voice was coated in honey, sprinkled with sugar.

Marjorie entered the sitting room of the queen of England, dressed in a green velvet gown with gold embroidery around the neckline and a matching green velvet French hood. She looked every bit a lady of the court, but Mary thought the green gown was a bit too reminiscent of Anne Boleyn. She looked down at the young girl with cold eyes, convinced she had traded her soul and faith for the accouterments.

Marjorie gave a deep curtsy. "Valorous evening, Your Majesty." Her head lowered respectfully.

Mary inspected the young girl's transformation from maid to lady. She could not pass up the opportunity to remark on it. "My, my, thou art lovely to behold," the queen said, wishing she had holy water to throw at the Devil's bride.

Marjorie stayed in her curtsy, as she had not yet been given permission to rise. "I most humbly thank you, Your Majesty."

Mary's lips twitched. "Rise." And Marjorie did, her hands folded.

"Dost thou see the bowl of berries and twigs?" Mary pointed with a flippant gesture to the Court of Dark's tribute that Awynn had provided her.

"I do."

"Viscount Awynn asked me to leave tribute to the pagans. Thou shalt tell him I did."

"Begging your pardon, my queen, wherefore dost thou need me to tell Viscount Awynn?"

The queen stood, fire raging in her eyes. *How dare this girl pretend she isn't a pawn in Satan's plot to claim my soul!*

"I am thy queen! Do not question me, wench! Viscount Awynn told me to leave tribute for those pagans!" Mary spat as she paced around the room, her belly bouncing with each step.

Marjorie kept her head down. Her hands shook.

Mary turned her eyes back to Marjorie. "Thou shalt tell him I did this or..." Abruptly, Mary lifted the lid of the trunk.

The body of one of Marjorie's beagles, Pansy, lay contorted, stuffed into the confined space.

Marjorie covered her mouth, stifling a scream.

"I shall kill thine other dogs if thou obey me not." Mary sneered as she stalked over to the fireplace and threw the tribute bowl and its contents into the fire. It flashed and raged. As the flames turned blue, both women cringed away from the hearth.

Mary turned back to Marjorie and spoke in a low growl, pointing to the floor. "Kneel before thy queen and swear thou wilt do as I say. Tell no one what thou hast seen or thine own body shall be in the box with the mongrels next." An unkind smile spread across her face as Marjorie knelt before her and pledged her allegiance. She swore to tell Awynn the queen had left the tribute. Mary dismissed the girl without a second glance.

As the queen prepared for bed, her window flew open, startling her. She held her belly as she felt the flutters of the baby kicking. Mary reached for a table to steady herself as the butterflies continued, her baby rolling with the sudden jolt. The queen caressed her stomach as she cooed to the somersaulting baby. She shuffled to bed, reciting her favorite prayer to the infant.

Marjorie exited the queen's privy chamber without a sound, avoiding the judgmental eyes of the guards. Shock was an astonishing companion in these situations. Being numb allowed Marjorie to function for the next precious moments under a shield of adrenaline and disconnection. The white taper candles cast a haze in the air, and she wondered if this was a dream or reality. But far away from the room and the guards, Marjorie's fortitude broke, the initial shock wearing off, and her body betrayed her. She shook uncontrollably; the tears would not stop. She slid down the wall, clutching at the stones for help, but they offered no support until the floor found her and stopped her descent. "What happened?" she murmured in between hiccupping sobs.

A clicking on the floors did not rouse Marjorie from her depression, even when Maisie and Daisy ran around the corner. The two beagles rarely journeyed this far into the palace. They found Marjorie in a crumpled mess on the floor. The beagles licked her tears away. She knew as she peered into their large brown eyes that they were searching for Pansy, but they would not find her. The image of Pansy's remains in the trunk almost broke Marjorie again. Instead, she stood, sniffling, wiping the dampness from her face, and ripped the hem of her linen underdressings to fashion makeshift leashes for the two dogs. She was not about to let them out of her sight. She tied the linen to their collars and allowed them to pull her down the hallway to Awynn's room. She placed her anger squarely on his shoulders, for hers carried far too much hurt to bear any more emotion. In her mind, he had a lot of explaining to do; after, she would take the dogs, and the three of them were leaving this place for good.

Marjorie did not bother to knock. She opened the door, and the dogs ran in first. She closed it fast, staring Awynn down.

"Marjorie, what is the matter?"

She knew she looked a mess with bloodshot eyes. Her hair fell into her eyes. She pushed it back away from her face, pondering her next move, because what he said next would determine how she handled things.

Her nostrils flared. "Wherefore did you ask the queen to leave tribute on the winter solstice? The lady is not a pagan! Are you a witch? Were you sent to convert our queen?" She zeroed in on him, demanding the truth.

"Marjorie, how didst thou know about this? Did Queen Mary—"

The beagles howled, a long, gut-wrenching sound regardless of species, conveying pain and heartbreak. They missed their sister. Marjorie froze listening to the beagles; she put her hands to her face and cried, dropping to the floor. She bowed her head and pounded the ground with her fists. She wanted to protect these innocent little creatures but knew blaming a person who had shown her nothing but kindness was not reasonable. He was not the source of her pain. The queen was, and lying for her was not an option for Marjorie. The girl's heart told her all she needed to know: Awynn was good, regardless of whether he read a Bible or not. The queen did, and she had killed an innocent creature. *So what if Awynn is a pagan? He acts more like a Christian than the queen.*

The queen had questioned and intimidated her. She had let the men in her court have their way with Marjorie because she was poor and a maid. Now she had killed one of the only creatures who had ever loved her. All because Awynn had asked her to leave out some berries.

Awynn observed Marjorie's pain, but he said nothing and he did not judge. She drew from his strength and finally stopped crying long enough to speak. "The lady killed mine own dog and commanded me to swear she left the tribute, but in truth, the lady burned it. The queen said if I did not swear, she would kill mine other dogs." Marjorie pointed a trembling finger at the beagles before dropping her head again, the sobs returning.

Every candle exploded. The fireplace transformed into an inferno. Marjorie's head shot up, and she looked around, eyes wide. She brought a hand to her lips.

"Marjorie, I am not a witch. I did not come here to convert your queen." Awynn spoke through gritted teeth. "Now, if we are done, take all the new clothing I bought you. Abandon anything from her. I will see to the dogs. We are departing now!"

Marjorie shivered, but did as he asked. Awynn explained he had already sent word to his queen about relocating Marjorie to a pagan group in Scotland that would teach her to be a healer. He was awaiting his queen's approval. But they were out of time.

As Marjorie readied her things, the windows blew open with a startling gust of cold air. The chambermaid jumped, letting out a frightened yip.

And that is my queen now. Always timely, Queen Aurora.

The paper landed on his window, completely undisturbed as the winds blew around it. It appeared like a bird waiting to be fed. The bright yellow wax seal was clear even in the dim candlelight. A septagram pressed into the wax. Awynn took the paper and cracked the seal. The scents of vanilla, lilac, and sunshine filled the room for a brief moment.

Awynn scanned the correspondence, then folded it.

"Dress warm. I have friends to take you someplace safe. You will be traveling for a bit. Wear the fur cloak."

Marjorie grabbed the blankets from the bed and used them to bundle up the beagles. Awynn threw in some of the leftover bread from their dinner. "Take this for the dogs. My friends will see you are fed on the way. We must go."

Awynn went to the door, but Marjorie put her hand on him, noticing he held no bags. "Will you not join us?" she asked, blanching.

He touched the back of his hand to her cheek. She held it to her face and pushed into it slightly, closing her eyes. "No, my dear. I have business to take care of here, but fear not, I will see you again. Remember what I said: all of the power and magick is within you, Marjorie. You are a good person, and you deserve happiness." He placed a chaste kiss on her forehead.

Marjorie kissed him back on the cheek. "Truly, I thank you."

Awynn led Marjorie out to the edges of the gardens, where a magnificent white stag waited. Behind him stood a glittering gilded sled led by four gigantic white deer. Marjorie stared in wonderment. "Those gents are magnificent!"

"Yes, they are." Awynn smiled. "They will take you to Scotland. A group will guide you, help you become a healer. You are talented, Marjorie, and your gift should be nurtured. You are under our protection now."

Marjorie tilted her head up to him as she settled into the sled, her fur cap framing her face. "You are mine opportunity, the one I did pray for," she said with a smile.

"Perhaps I am," he whispered as the sled took off.

Awynn was certain Theadova and his Aubane Faction would carry Marjorie to safety. But as the golden silhouette of the sleigh vanished over the dark horizon, his smile disintegrated. The snow melted around him. His Tudor clothes smoldered and smoked until fabric fell to the ground in tatters. He shimmered, and Viscount Awynn dissolved into Bishop Awynn in all his height and glory. Once again, he wore his white bishop's uniform, and the blood-red underside of his cape billowed in the breeze. From his boot he drew a small ash wand. He tapped it against his palm, and it grew into a six-foot staff topped with a large yellow topaz crystal.

"Now, Queen Mary, we have some unfinished business," Awynn growled as he marched back to the castle, steam rising off him. His boots melted the thick snow to the cobblestone with each step he took.

Chapter Sixteen:
FLY, LOS, FLY
(DECEMBER 21, 1554)

Los concealed himself outside the human monarch's window. He had been there for longer than he liked. At first, there was nothing to report. He had passed the time by pretending to be a gargoyle, which he had found amusing, striking different poses perched atop the tower ledge. He measured the size of his wings next to the stone gargoyles and chuckled when he discovered that his were bigger. He marched across the ledge, mocking the gargoyles, unfurling his wings to show off, his snorts becoming louder.

Los watched the winter sky change. The moon peeked out from behind the grey clouds, casting a silver glow on the snow; it sparkled and twinkled as if the stars had fallen to the ground and buried themselves in the white blanket below. Snow was not something dragons saw much of, even the ice dragons. Los thought about flying down and playing in it just to feel the cool powder on his body, but he knew better than to leave his post. Instead, he settled for listening to the crunch of the snow beneath his claws as he traversed the ledges.

Contrary to popular belief, dragons were not cold-blooded creatures. They ran hotter than most, even the ice dragons—it took a lot of energy to make acid, fire, or ice. Their high metabolism created heat. In Los's case, his unique chameleon-like ability also caused a rise in body temperature.

Los continued to play with his stone cousins, making funny faces and scary stances, until he heard a creature whining and whimpering. The sound flowed from the top of the arch window. The glass was tilted, facing outward; it would be a tight fit. He tucked his wings close and slipped into the window. In an instant, Los was the color of the walls in Queen Mary's room. The tall window was a vent for any excess smoke from the fireplace. Los's claws dug into the walls as he observed where the sounds were originating.

A small furry creature half the size of Los had a strap around her neck and seemed to be embroiled in a fight for her life. A woman screamed commands over the din. Los heard the group of humans call the captured animal a mongrel, a dog, and a beast. *These humans must not understand what a beast really is.* Much to his surprise, he could understand the animal, not in words so much as emotions. She was called Pansy, she had two siblings, and she was a good girl. She knew the lady yelling at her did not like her. The lady was the queen, who was yelling at the man to "keep it still!"

What the humans heard as whining was Pansy begging to find the human girl she loved very much.

The queen drew a sword, and Pansy went into survival mode, snapping her teeth at the queen. Los wanted to intervene but knew he could not. A second later, Pansy took her final breath, and her last thoughts were of love for her human. Los closed his eyes as the queen threw the sword down and told the man what to do with the "mongrel's body." Los wished he was like Dragor so he could burn the humans right where they stood. He understood why Jarvok had kept him away from humans: they were animals with no respect for life of any kind.

The queen turned to the side, and Los's eyes widened. *She is with child! Yet, she killed with no remorse. The poor child will be born with ice in its veins. Maybe the queen's father was cruel too?* If that were the case, Los could not blame her, not really. However, the child she was carrying was part Fae; Los could only hope that would override the human deficiencies and break the cycle.

The queen changed into her nightclothes and went about her business as if nothing out of the ordinary had happened. Staying in stealth mode, watching and waiting, Los saw the bowl holding the tribute. He sensed the Fire Drake's energy signature from across the room. He looked at the window and counted about twenty paces from the table to where the bowl sat by the window. Twenty paces separated the queen from doing the right thing and inciting war between the two Fae courts. Los knew Jarvok all too well, and if Queen Aurora did not take the baby immediately, the Dark Fae king would go in as hot as Dragor's molten heart, spouting acid like Raycor.

The queen sat down and kicked the box holding Pansy's body. Los held his stomach and swallowed, belching as his insides churned.

A pretty human girl in a green dress entered the room. Los could sense she was nervous, even scared. The queen was not very nice to the girl. Los recognized the Fire Drake's name, and they talked about the tribute. Then, the queen showed the human girl Pansy's body. His heart sank for her. The poor girl was pale, and Los's rage rose again. His hope—that the baby might break the cycle of cruelty—was eviscerated.

The queen burned the tribute.

Los had to leave, for if he did not, he would kill the queen himself. She had murdered a small dog and put his kin at risk. He had finished his mission. The small dragon tipped the window open and slid out. The queen looked up over her shoulder, startled. Los jumped from the window and hurtled toward the ground, his wings pinned to his body. He resembled an arrow's head, his eyes protected by a thin, transparent membrane that allowed him to see but kept the wind and debris from entering them. He opened his wings and caught an updraft, propelling him aloft. Los banked and headed toward the meeting spot he and Zion had agreed upon.

Los was not as graceful as the other dragons; his flight patterns were jerky, and he never made it up into the atmosphere above the clouds like Fornia or Dragor. However, Los was able to weave in and out between the trees, something the bigger dragons could never do. The faster Los flew, the angrier he got. He desired revenge, and he wanted it now. He had been surprised he could understand Pansy and now wished he had brought her some comfort in her last moments. He wanted to tell her he would avenge her.

Los banked right and headed back toward Hampton Court, determined to somehow bring Pansy peace.

Chapter Seventeen:
DON'T PISS OFF THE FAE
(DECEMBER 21, 1554, 11:57 P.M.)

B ishop Awynn strode into Hampton Court Palace. He had no regard for how he looked—it was just before midnight, and only the guards were still up. He placed a cloak over his bishop's uniform, but left his face unchanged, though he hunched quite a bit to disguise his height. No one paid him much mind.

He did find a stable boy wandering around. "Boy, dost thou know the baker, Stella?"

"Aye, my lord."

"I need you to go to her room and give her this package from Viscount Awynn and her cousin Marjorie. Make sure you wake her up and hand her the package personally. This is for your troubles." Awynn handed the boy a tip and a package wrapped in brown paper. "There will be a special tip for you in the viscount's room when the job is done."

The package contained money, the deed to a bakery in Glasgow, and a letter from a benefactor who believed in her talents; the catch was she had to leave tonight and tell no one. He had made all the arrangements to make sure the queen did not retaliate against her as well. The boy gave Awynn a big smile and took off running.

Awynn returned to his room and used the fireplace to find his way into Queen Mary's privy chambers. The chimes sounded, sealing Mary's fate. The fire roared to life as he stepped out from the blaze. The queen was sound asleep in her bedchamber. A guard keeping watch outside her bedroom door sprang to life, and Awynn knocked him out with his staff. Awynn opened the chamber doors, and another guard met him, ready to engage, but Awynn was a master with his staff, wielding it as a weapon. The guard did not stand a chance.

The bishop pulled the drapes back from Queen Mary's bed and raised his arms, igniting every candle in the room. The fireplace erupted into a firestorm, belching sparks. The room was so bright, it looked like the sun was high in the sky on a summer's day.

"Open your eyes, Mary! I know you are awake." Awynn's voice echoed, filling the room.

The queen stirred and yawned. "Viscount Awynn, 'tis a pleasure." It was the same sugary-sweet tone she had used when they first met.

"It is Bishop Awynn to you. Did you leave your tribute?" He tilted his head.

"Whatever dost thou mean?" she cooed with her eyes wide, blinking innocently.

"Do not play games with me, woman."

Mary's tone changed, and the sugar vanished as if dissolved in water. "What if I did or did not?" The queen tightened her lips and folded her arms across her chest.

"Did you kill one of Marjorie's dogs and threaten to kill the others if she did not lie for you?"

Mary sneered. "Mine agreement is with thy queen. I do not answer to thee."

"You are correct. Your agreement is with Queen Aurora. I am merely her representative. But make no mistake, Mary, my queen is not a forgiving one; just ask your father. Queen Aurora will tell you all about him when she sees you. And she will see you. What I can do is rescind the Court of Light's invitation and protection, as an acting emissary of my kin."

Mary yawned, patting her mouth.

Awynn raised his staff, the crystal flickered indicating the rise in his energy. "You, Queen Mary, are no longer welcome in the Veil or in the Court of Light. I formally rescind your invitation."

The queen scoffed. "I'm carrying a babe who is half Fae." She smiled as if she had found a loophole and fixed her blankets as if preparing herself to go back to sleep.

"For now you are," Awynn said, raising an eyebrow at her.

Mary threw the covers off, jumped from her bed, and dropped to her knees. "Prithee do not take my babe. Prithee, I am sorry." She clung to his leg with the strength of a boa constrictor.

He batted her away with the back of his hand. "Now you want to apologize. It is too late; as you said: the agreement is not with me. I have no say. Oh, and Mary? Marjorie is under my protection, so do not even think of retaliating against her or her cousin. If you do, I will see it as a personal attack, and you have seen what my fire is capable of." With a flick of his wrist, Awynn sent a spark from a candle to an ancient tapestry, and it went up like kindling.

Mary gasped. Cradling her head, she fell to the side and clutched her midsection, wailing.

As Awynn exited the room, he heard a scraping from the sitting room. A trunk was moving across the floor all by itself. Between Mary's overly dramatic sobs and the trunk, he was getting a headache. The trunk headed toward a low window, and it seemed to want to go up and out, but it was having some trouble.

"Do you need help?" he asked. The trunk dropped with a thud. Awynn inspected the trunk and waved his staff around it, then opened the lid. A breeze from behind him lifted his hair. Awynn recognized Pansy's body and lowered his head as tears fell for the dog. Then he felt a presence and spun around.

A small amber-and-black-speckled dragon the size of a red wolf materialized. The dragon's horn feathers were wilted, and his tongue lolled out of the side of his mouth. The creature moved in front of the trunk, blocking Awynn. The bishop stepped back as the dragon glanced at Pansy and closed the trunk with his tail. His large, glassy eyes focused on Awynn. His wings curled around him, his ears and their black feathers pinned back, his tail tucked to the side with only the tip slightly waving as if sensing the air. Awynn didn't see aggressive intent behind his gaze.

"What are you doing here?" *You are far too small of a dragon to be out alone on the solstice; you must be a spy for the Dark Fae king.*

Los pointed to the trunk and to Mary's bedroom, acting out what he had seen. Awynn nodded, following along. "You witnessed her cruelty, didn't you?"

The dragon bobbed his head up and down.

"You were trying to take the body from here, weren't you?"

The dragon lifted his head back and chortled.

"That is very nice of you. I will help. I can transport the trunk with me. Meet me in the gardens, and we will bury her together. All right?"

The dragon jumped to the window and vanished. "Well, I'll take that as a yes." Awynn lifted the trunk with ease and used the fire to leave the room.

A few minutes later, the unlikely pair stood at the farthest point of the castle's grounds. The spot where Marjorie and the dogs had had their snowball fight a day ago seemed fitting. Awynn had grabbed a shovel from the stable as he walked to the chosen point. He dug a hole as Los helped with his claws. Awynn laid Pansy down, gently wrapped in a blanket from the palace. He and the dragon stood in silence for a few breaths. The two Fae shed tears over the loss of a creature who had loved unselfishly and was taken selfishly. Then Awynn and the dragon filled the hole, and the two parted ways, heading back to their respective courts, separated by their loyalties but bound by this small act.

Chapter Eighteen:
REACTION VERSUS ACTION
(DECEMBER 22, 12:15 AM)

L os slipped in and out of tree branches, cutting through the crisp winter night's air to the meeting place Zion had chosen. He did not spin or somersault like he normally did during high-speed flights. A more somber disposition had overtaken him during his journey back. Aerial acrobatics did not seem respectful after what he had witnessed. Los touched down in the open field without a word to Zion and Raycor, who were waiting for him. "By all that is light in the Universe, Los! We are late! Hop on. I can't have you lagging behind anymore." Los mounted the larger Acid-Breather and huddled up for the ride back to Blood Haven.

Los's tardiness made for an unhappy Zion, but the events of the evening had made the small dragon apathetic. He let Zion grumble about his delay without so much as a huff or a snort.

Raycor, on the other hand, was well aware something was off with the smaller dragon but knew to leave well enough alone. She bucked at Zion a few times, hoping her rider would get the hint, but alas, Zion could be thick-headed when he was delayed, and this was no exception.

The group arrived at Blood Haven with Zion still lecturing Los."...When Jarvok sends you on these missions, you need to be more efficient. What were you doing? Playing with the gargoyles, I would bet my left gauntlet! You better not have defiled anything! How are you going to expect to go on more of these if you can't meet at the rendezvous point on time! That's the first thing we learned in Power Brigade training..." Zion glanced over his shoulder to look at the small dragon, but Los remained stoic.

They landed and Los remained quiet. No witty banter or even an eye roll escaped him, very uncharacteristic of Los.

Zion poked the miniature dragon before they knocked on the large double doors. "Well? Did she leave the tribute?"

Los rolled his eyes and lumbered through the doors, ignoring Zion completely.

That was more like him, Zion thought.

"You are late," Jarvok said as Los walked to his king and bowed his head. "Do you have a report for me?"

Zion stepped aside, giving Los the floor. The dragon chortled, gurgled, snorted, and ticked his way through his conversation with the king.

"The human queen did not leave tribute. Los, is the Court of Light aware of it? Was the queen pregnant when you left her?" Jarvok asked the dragon. "Do you believe they will retaliate against the queen of England?" Jarvok was inches away from the dragon now.

With all the attention on him, the little dragon thought it would be easier to put on a show than explain things. Placing his claws away from his stomach, he mimed a belly. He walked around with his hand in the air, swaying his hips side to side, wagging his finger about, as though he were the queen. Next Los grabbed his own neck and pretended to squeeze.

"I would say that is a most definite yes to both questions, my liege," Zion remarked.

Los continued his dramatics and fell to the floor playing dead, tongue lolling out of his mouth. The dragon opened one eye to see if Jarvok was watching.

"Maybe we should applaud?" Zion said with his hand to his mouth.

"Well done!" Jarvok gave a jovial laugh and clapped.

The dragon stood, bowed, and floated up a few feet, smirking.

"Prepare Lieutenant Asa and a few members of the High Council Guard: Yagora and Pria. We are going to pay Queen Aurora a visit. She is in violation of the treaty. This is disrespectful to us, and as of now, the human is still with child. Aurora did not terminate the pregnancy. She is complicit in our humiliation." Jarvok snatched his helmet off the table, causing the small models to fall.

"Perhaps we should give her a day or so to act on it. In all actuality, it has only been a few hours, my liege. She might not have been informed yet," Zion said, trying to keep his king from reacting impulsively.

"No! This should have already been dealt with! I would have struck the human down, yet Aurora is being passive and showing far too much compassion. We go now."

Los nodded and shook his head, trying to convey his agreement with Zion, but Jarvok, in his stubbornness, patted the dragon. "Glad we are thinking alike, Los."

The chameleon dragon chortled and dropped his head, his ear feathers drooping. Zion shrugged but followed behind his king.

Chapter Nineteen:
Compassion
(December 22, 1554, 1:15 a.m.)

A rriving at the Court of Light, Awynn sent for the other bishops and gathered them in the queen's private meeting quarters. It did not come as a surprise to anyone that Queen Mary was being difficult. Awynn described his time in her court, including her attempt to blackmail the chambermaid by threatening her dogs. The shock settled in from Mary's blatant disregard for life.

"Poor creature. Did Mary display even an ounce of remorse?" Aurora could not fathom why she had aided the human queen in the first place. However, deep down, Aurora knew why. Her own abandonment issues with their Creator made her amenable to the English monarch. Aurora related Mary's hardships with her father, King Henry, to her own with her Creator. This blinded the Fae queen to the fact Mary was never to be trusted.

The sound of Awynn's voice helped Aurora focus on the here-and-now. There must be repercussions. "Mary never admitted to committing the act to me, Your Grace," Awynn said. "She disclosed the information to Marjorie, but I did find the body of the animal in her room with the assistance of a dragon from the Court of Dark."

Bishop Geddes huffed, flailing his arms. "Well, this is just perfect, Bishop Awynn. This means they know the human oaf did not leave tribute. You should have led with that! Not the story about the stupid mongrel!" Geddes spat out the words, his fist striking the table.

Aurora's wings emerged, and the wind picked up in the room, making everyone privy to her agitation. "Geddes! The animal lost its light in our name. How dare you!" She pounded both fists down on the table and leaned forward. Her turquoise eyes flashed green as they bored into her senior advisor.

"Forgive me, Your Grace, it is the stress of the events." He looked downward, but his lack of sincere piety was not lost on his queen. She glared at him until he uttered several more "Forgive me's."

Aurora turned her attention back to Awynn. "The Court of Dark will be a problem. They will want retribution for this insult—"

A sudden heavy knocking communicated a new urgency. Desdemona called from the other side of the door, "Your Grace? We have a situation!"

Aurora flicked her wrist, and the doors opened. Desdemona stood straight-backed, ready to report.

"King Jarvok and four of his companions are demanding an audience with you now. They are outside the palace bridge."

Aurora, looking to the ceiling, shook her head. "So much for having time to prepare. Let them into the Great

Hall, but the dragons stay outside. Those are my terms. I will be right down."

Desdemona bowed and ran to deliver her queen's wishes.

"Well, my bishops, it seems we will have to deal with this right now. So you are aware, I intend to terminate our agreement with the queen of England before the moon rises. I will make it most unpleasant. Awynn, you have already rescinded our invitation and protection?"

"Yes, Your Grace."

She nodded at him and extended her hand toward the door. "Then all we have left to do is explain to King Jarvok that we are handling this in line with the treaty, along with finding the Dinay Mera clan a new host. Let us go greet our unexpected guests."

Bishop Ward stopped mid-procession, giving his queen the once-over. "But Your Grace, you are not ready to receive them. Your gown and the lack of a crown are not appropriate for their audience."

Aurora held her hands out to her sides, examining her cream gown. "You are beginning to sound like Ungarra, Bishop Ward. While I may not have my crown on at this very moment, I do not think anyone will question exactly who is the queen of the Court of Light." Her eyes glowed as she spoke. "Let us not keep the king waiting."

The Great Hall came to life, glittering in the moonlight as Will-o-Wisps flittered about, lighting the large quartz candelabras hanging from the geometric ceiling. Each one dropped down with large circular tiers like a celebratory cake. Hundreds of thick pillar candles decorated the descending tiers, all in pale pastel colors representing the Chakras. Candles in hues of red, yellow, orange, green, blue, indigo, and violet smoldered, then sprang to life, illuminating the Great Hall as their whispers of color played off the quartz floor and crystal walls. Aurora's crystal throne with the septagram as its crowning glory sat cold and alone atop a platform. Seven large stairs led to the throne; it might as well have been a mountain.

King Jarvok and his party shuffled into the Great Hall, escorted by the Royal Guards. *All present and accounted for.* The guards took their places about the room, encircling their "guests" on the tiered stairs, giving these guards the advantage of higher ground. They were armed with bows and arrows, while the ground level guards had spears. The Dark Fae looked around the expansive hall, trying to keep their mouths closed. This was their first time inside the Court of Light. They all shifted uneasily, the brightness hitting home. The Power Brigade Angels had never been allowed inside the upper levels of the Shining Kingdom.

Jarvok gazed up at the lotus design in the ceiling, his face placid. *Is this what it was like to be loved by the Creator? Is this what they left behind?* Reality crashed into him as the clicks of boots sounded, and the familiar call of power wafted through the room.

Queen Aurora had arrived with her four bishops. She glanced around, positive the Illuminasqua were hiding in the Great Hall ready for action should the situation call for it. Aurora contemplated calling the four Guardians but thought better of it. She did not want to escalate the situation, fearing it might be interpreted as an act of aggression. She took her throne and welcomed King Jarvok, his lieutenants, and two members of his High Council Guard, though her gaze lingered on Yagora for an extra second. Their encounter was so very long ago, yet it was still an open sore. Aurora had embarrassed Yagora and outwitted her. However, the queen had carried the burden of their run-in for centuries, her kin often paying the price. Yagora had made it a priority to torture many members of the Court of Light during the war. Speculation was that Yagora had done this in retaliation for her defeat by Aurora at the Red Sea.

"Merry Meet, King Jarvok. I am aware of Queen Mary of England's unfortunate choice to disregard the terms of our agreement. I can assure you, I am handling her disrespectful gesture."

King Jarvok placed a kyanite boot on the first step leading to the throne. Two guards drew their crystal-and-iron-dipped spears, creating an X blocking his path. His honey eyes smoldered through the spears, his top lip pulled back as he sneered. "You can assure me of nothing! The human woman is still with child. A second after she refused to leave tribute was a second too long in the eyes of the Court of Dark." Jarvok made a fist as he punched the air downward for emphasis.

Queen Aurora stood from her throne, trying to keep her temper in check. Her hair danced around her like a candle in the wind. "King Jarvok, I understand your frustration. I am unhappy with her decision to act in an uncooperative manner." Aurora's voice deepened, her eyes focusing on the Dark Fae king. "This lack of respect is an insult to both courts and will be dealt with accordingly."

Jarvok did not move from the step. "Frustration? Do not placate me, little queen. You are no longer a Virtue. Do not act as though you hold authority over me or my kin." Jarvok's lip twitched. "Your solution is not satisfactory! The treaty strictly forbade one court being favored over another. You are in violation of the treaty."

Wind swirled in the Great Hall. The hanging chandeliers swayed under the vaulted ceiling. "We were both denied tribute, King Jarvok! One side was not favored over another. I am not in violation of the treaty. Watch how you sling your mud, King of the Dark." The Light Fae queen tilted her chin up; her shoulders were squared with righteousness as she bladed her body, taking a defensive stance.

Jarvok was undeterred by her warning. "Or what?" he whispered in a low growl. Zion, Asa, Yagora, and Pria all tensed beside their king, ready for whatever might happen next. The Royal Guards on the tiers raised their bows and arrows, surrounding the Dark Fae, poised for a confrontation.

"Do not test me, King Jarvok," Aurora said in a calm, steady voice, her hand extended as if stopping him from making an impulsive move.

Asa, as the Court of Dark's Seer, reached out with her scrying abilities to sense the extra bodies of Fae who could not be seen with the naked eye. She felt at least another twenty-five energetic signatures above them. "Illuminasqua," she whispered. Between them, two hundred Royal Guards, four elemental bishops, Desdemona, and one queen there was no way for the five of them to fight without major losses or injuries. Asa reached out to the queen, aligned her Chakras, and focused on the indigo light at her forehead. The light grew as she visualized a two-petal lotus flower opening up in between her eyebrows. The Dark Fae repeated "*Ajna*," tapping into her third eye. She needed all the help she could get to break through Queen Aurora's shields.

A flood of intentions hit her. Asa's eyes flashed white, and she knew Aurora meant what she said; the queen planned on dealing with Queen Mary as soon as possible. The feelings faded, and Asa subtly shifted on her feet for a second. "My liege, a word, please?"

"Yes, Lieutenant?" He did not take his eyes off the scene unfolding around him, backing up to listen to his seer and third lieutenant.

"The queen is true to her word. Perhaps we should grant her a period to enact her plan. After all, she is correct. She is technically not in violation of the treaty. If the human monarch did not leave tribute for the Court of Dark, she was not going to leave it for the Court of Light either during the summer solstice."

Jarvok gave a sideways glance at Aurora, whose smug look did not bode well for Asa. The queen had overheard their conversation and was not above gloating. "I would listen to your seer, King Jarvok. It seems she read the contract and comprehended it. Take your dragons and begone. Let me handle the important issues." Her trivializing flip of the wrist unintentionally sealed Asa's fate as it inflamed the Dark Fae king. Jarvok's left eye twitched. He was mortified that he appeared uneducated, especially since he had analyzed the contract, which he believed Aurora had been ignorant in drawing up. Moreover, he despised being dismissed. The Dark Fae king looked petty, vindictive, and tempestuous, which he played into whether he realized it or not.

Zion noticed his king's tell and lifted his head to the sky in a silent gesture for strength. He recognized what was to come. Asa should have quit with the first sentence, and Zion knew how Jarvok would react; he would blame her for this. He grumbled, readying himself.

Jarvok drew his hand back to strike his third-in-command for her insolence in correcting him in front of the Light Fae queen. Though, it was more about *Aurora* insulting him. Zion rolled his eyes and exhaled as he "bumped" into his king's shoulder, rolling him forward to the ground.

Zion pinned Jarvok down to keep him from hitting Asa, disguising it as a protective measure. "My liege!" Zion called out as the circle of Dark Fae, closed in on Jarvok with their backs to their king, assessing the risk of the room, fearing for his safety.

"My liege, please listen to Asa. Do not incite a war unnecessarily—at least consult with Lady Zarya. Do not give this queen any more of a reason to act above us. If she is so sure of her plan, strike a deal," Zion whispered into his king's ear, trying to soothe his bruised ego.

Jarvok harrumphed, indicating he wanted Zion off and the others to give him space. By the time the Dark Fae backed up, the Royal Guards were even more confused and edgy. However, Jarvok knew what Zion had done; he shot his second-in-command and Asa a sour look.

Zion knew he would pay for this later, but if it saved Asa from a beating she did not deserve, and his king from appearing like a Goblin's ass, it was well worth it to him. Jarvok was a good Fae, but there were times he could not shake their old ways from the Brigade. *Never disrespect your commanding officer in front of the enemy, even when they are wrong.*

The few moments had helped to keep the situation from going in a bad direction. Zion gave Asa a wink as they stood.

"Forgive me, my liege. I thought I saw a guard flinch. I was mistaken," Zion said with a bow.

Aurora cleared her throat, drawing their attention back to her. "If you are all finished, I would like to end this visit. I will terminate Mary's contract by tomorrow's eve. Is that satisfactory with you, King Jarvok?" Aurora said, very much composed.

Jarvok glanced at Asa, who gave a subtle nod. "I would like a contract written between us stating you will do so, or I will receive some retribution."

"Very well. I will agree. Do I need to call the Oracles, or can we get on with this, King Jarvok?"

"I will not bother Lady Zarya with this matter, for if you do not follow through, I will return with my dragons." His eyes glinted threateningly

Aurora shook her head and brought her hand to her temple. "Threats are not necessary, King Jarvok. I have every intention of keeping my word."

Jarvok only stared.

Awynn volunteered to act as witness to this new agreement since he had initially brokered the deal with Queen Mary. As Queen Aurora drew the conditions up, she spoke them aloud to King Jarvok. "This states I have until the sun sets and the moon rises tomorrow to terminate Queen Mary's pregnancy. Once I do, the contract between her and I will be null and void, thus fulfilling my obligation to the Court of Dark. Is this satisfactory to you, King Jarvok?"

King Jarvok gestured to see the parchment for himself. "And if you do not meet the timeline stated?"

"What do you feel is a fair reprisal? Not that it will be an issue," Aurora said, glancing at Awynn who stood to Jarvok's left.

"Territory," the king replied.

Aurora arched an eyebrow. "Enlighten me, King Jarvok."

"If you do not meet the timeline, you will give up an area with your worshippers, turning them and the temple over to the Court of Dark." Jarvok's silken voice practically sang with victory.

"Name the territory now," Aurora said, impatience ringing in her voice.

"The Stone Coven."

"Done," Aurora said without a second thought.

Bishop Geddes spoke up. "Your Grace, no!"

Aurora held her hand up to the bishop. "Bishop Geddes, my word is my bond," she said, her cold stare drilling into Jarvok's eyes. Her gaze was a mix of confidence in her decision and mistrust in her royal counterpart. "Bishop Awynn, make the adjustment. King Jarvok will sign the contract; I will sign after."

Awynn amended the contract and handed Jarvok a Galena blade, but the king unsheathed his Elestial Blade to draw blood instead.

Whether it was the stress of the situation, the earlier incident with Zion, or the new guard, no one knew. As King Jarvok unsheathed his auric blade, a guard panicked and let his Black tourmaline-and-iron dipped arrow fly at King Jarvok. Time stood still. The hum of the arrow cut through the air. If Zion had not cried wolf earlier, perhaps Jarvok would have taken him seriously, but while Zion screamed for his king, Jarvok stood his ground.

The second-in-command of the Dark Fae struggled to reach Jarvok. Even while the world around Jarvok spun and swirled into action, he remained stoic. Yagora and Pria were powerless to stop the events unfolding with such speed that the two High Council Guard members were forced to watch the arrow find its landing spot.

Zion did not make it to Jarvok in time. The arrow pierced flesh, and a sickening gulp and gurgling sound reverberated throughout the Great Hall.

Jarvok closed his eyes tightly in shock and horror as slick, warm liquid seeped over his skin. He wiped at the blood on his face and felt his torso for a wound, but found nothing. The blood splatter had come from Bishop Awynn. The Fae wavered directly in front of Jarvok, his eyes clouding over, losing focus. As the bishop fell forward, Jarvok instinctively caught him; Awynn clutched for the Dark Fae king's shoulders. He sank heavily to his knees, the arrow sticking out of his back. Zion and Asa threw the Royal Guards aside on the way to their king. They pulled Jarvok away as Aurora ran to Awynn. Desdemona descended upon the trigger-happy guard.

The Dark Fae were astonished that the Light Fae Bishop had taken an arrow meant for their king. Aurora and the other bishops surrounded Awynn, trying to stop the bleeding. Bishop Caer cleansed the wound with water, using his elemental gift, but it was far too late; the arrow had pierced his heart. Every Fae saw his light fading fast.

"Get Lady Ambia!" a Fae yelled.

Awynn coughed, and blood poured from his mouth. He reached for his queen, calling for her."Auror—" Awynn struggled. His breath was thready, his voice reedy.

Aurora gathered him in her lap, cradling him. "Shh, do not talk. We are getting Lady Ambia. Save your strength." Her eyes were full of tears. She had so many questions. *Why did he do it? He could have just incinerated the arrow or yelled for Jarvok to move. Anything but this.*

"Please...listen—" he coughed. "I do not have much time. My light is almost gone." More blood trickled from his lips. His white uniform was covered in rivulets of blue.

"No. Do not say such things," Aurora whispered, brushing his hair from his face, only to smear more blood. "You will be fine." Her hands shook.

"My queen, lies do not become us." He tried to smile but coughed again. More blue blood streaked his white hair, staining it a sickly pale grey. The other bishops exchanged glances. Aurora slowly nodded, admitting defeat.

"To serve you has been my honor," Awynn choked out. "You are a good queen. I have learned so much among the humans, most of all about compassion, and you too must learn it." *Cough.* "Compassion can build a bridge that hate has burned. It transcends all species. It speaks all languages without saying a word. Compassion can heal what ails the heart, make the blind see through their rage, make the deaf hear reason, and let those who are mute speak their truth." *Cough.* "Compassion is an act, not an emotion. Everyone has a story. Hatred is made, not born, so do not nurture it; extinguish it with compassion. Remember this, Aurora, for as queen you lead by example. I wish I could have given you more." His head dangled to the side, and there was a slow, low exhale.

Aurora bent her head to his chest and cried. A ray of light emanated from the center of Awynn's body—bright yellow. Desdemona swooped in and grabbed her queen, dragging her from the body. They watched as swirling spheres of energy lit up, starting at his groin area with a red glow; then his naval, which was yellow; followed by orange at his solar plexus; green by the middle of his chest; blue at his throat; indigo at his forehead; and purple at the crown of his head. All of his Chakras spun in perfect sync with each other. A white light bloomed from their symmetry, a blending of colors that blossomed into a lotus flower, cocooning Awynn's body. Aurora reached out, but Desdemona pulled the queen back again, pinning her arms and hugging her. In a flash of white light, the flower closed around him, and his body vanished. What remained was a vibrant translucent rainbow, slowly dissipating.

Pria and Yagora gasped and fell to their knees.

"Where is he?" Aurora screamed repeatedly.

Jarvok looked at his kin. "Answer her if you know." His voice was quiet but stern.

Yagora glanced at Pria, who stood and walked over to the queen of the Court of Light. "He has reached the Rainbow Body, a level of self-realization I have only seen one human worshipper reach. It is a state of complete oneness with the universal energies. I did not know it was possible for our kind. May I ask? Was he created of Angelic lineage or was he born of the Earth?"

Aurora swallowed and wiped away her tears. "Awynn was my first bishop born of the Earth and the last Fire Drake." There was an edge of anger to her voice.

Pria nodded in understanding. "If he was born of the Earth, it may be why he was able to reach that level. He is literally one with the universe and the light." She raised her head upward, her lips moving in silent words.

With that, Pria stepped back to join King Jarvok.

"Thank you, Pria," Aurora said, her spine straightening. "King Jarvok, given what has transpired, I ask for time to grieve the passing of my bishop. Fae blood has been spilled. Our contract is null. I will take care of Mary as I hold her responsible for this travesty. I ask to enact revenge as I see fit, but my original timetable no longer holds true. You can return to the Court of Light on her due date to witness if the retribution is adequate. If not, the Stone Coven is yours." Aurora's tone did not ask for a challenge. Bishop Geddes grimaced at her words but said nothing.

Considering her bishop had just saved his life, Jarvok did not have room to argue. "I am sorry for your loss, Queen Aurora. Your terms are acceptable to me. I will return on the human monarch's delivery date to see the contract terminated. Once again, I am sorry blood has been spilled. We will take our leave." Jarvok gestured for his kin, who followed him out single file. The Dark Fae placed their first three fingers to their lips in the Power Brigade's universal sign for respect in grief; there was nothing to say to make this right. Silence was best.

Aurora said nothing as the Court of Dark exited the Great Hall. Once they were gone, she asked for the guard who had shot the arrow.

Desdemona brought him to her. He knelt before his queen, trembling and crying.

Aurora had considered executing him, but as she stared into the Fae's lilac eyes, saw his pale-amethyst skin and the four gold hoops in his forehead, she understood he was young; the number of hoops indicated he was just one hundred years old. Awynn's words about compassion reverberated in her head. The guard whimpered. "I am sorry, my queen. Please forgive me." He wept, and she held his shaking hands in hers.

"You are forgiven. However, Captain Desdemona will take your weapon until she feels you are more at ease with it." Aurora gestured to Desdemona, who led the Fae away.

Aurora walked to her throne and turned to address the silent room. "We have lost the last Fire Drake. Bishop Awynn has met his Oblivion while in service to the Court of Light. He made a choice to protect his fellow Fae. We can all learn from his sacrifice." The sprinkling of blue blood on her dress caught her eye, the pattern of spray uneven around her waist. *These are remnants of his words and his last moments on Earth.* She concentrated on her hands, stained blue. The floor was streaked with his essence. *Awynn. Blood, so much blood, but no body. He is gone.* "Bishop Awynn was an exemplary Fae. He will be missed. Fire lilies will be placed in the Moon Garden in honor of him and in the water channels around the palace. Ring the bells in the key of E, three times for his element." Aurora's eyes were a mix of tears with moments of anger flashing in between. Fire and ice—like Awynn.

"Make no mistake, my kin. The human monarch, Queen Mary of England, will pay dearly for this. Awynn's blood is on her hands, and I will avenge him. You have my word."

Chapter Twenty:
"My Word Is My Bond"
(December 22, 1554, 4:00 a.m.)

Queen Mary awoke, startled by her bedroom shutters blowing open. Her canopy's drapes whistled and rustled around her. She looked to her privy chamber guard, who was fast asleep despite the commotion. She took her slipper and threw it, hitting him upon the head, yet the guard did not move. Queen Mary got out of bed and poked at his shoulder, but still nothing. He snored.

"By Lucifer's own," she exclaimed.

A woman's voice echoed from the window of Mary's bedroom. "No, not a demon, Mary, but when I am done, you won't be able to tell the difference."

Mary yelled, "Guards! Where are my guards?"

The voice spoke again, soft as silk. "They aren't coming to help you, Mary. No one is."

Mary ran to the door, but a gust of wind knocked her to her knees. She lay pinned to the floor by an unseen force. There were no footsteps, but Mary felt her assailant creeping closer. Suddenly, she found herself lifted up and flipped roughly onto her back. A shadow loomed; she felt eyes on her, staring down.

"Prithee, I am with child," Mary whimpered, reaching for her stomach.

The other woman laughed. "Oh, I know you are. I helped put the babe in your womb. I believe you said you were eternally grateful to me." Her tone was laced with disapproval. Mary's eyes grew wide. Her attacker was the same woman she had called her savior months earlier.

Queen Aurora hovered over Mary, her energy wings twice the length of her body. Her crimson hair danced like fire around her. Aurora's eyes blazed emerald green with power, and from her skin emanated a glow one only saw when the Fae queen was furious. Aurora folded her arms before she fell forward, stopping inches from Mary's face as she lay restrained on the floor. Aurora smiled. "Your dishonesty runs deep, from father to daughter and beyond. You shall not corrupt another baby swan." Aurora placed her right hand over Mary's swollen belly and spoke in a voice which held the power of a thousand stars, "*You are free to fly, Little One. You are free to soar; you are bound to this vessel no more.*" Aurora's eyes were now squarely focused on the other queen, and the energy in her voice called for vengeance. "*My word is my bond; you have not honored yours. We are friends no more. As it is above, so it is below.*" Aurora took her hand away from the human queen.

Mary's belly clenched, but all the English monarch felt was the warm tears falling from her eyes. Aurora lightly wiped the tears away. To Mary's credit, she did not recoil from Aurora's touch or even flinch.

Stoicism, an interesting tactic. Aurora whispered into Mary's ear, "Awynn's passing was quick, and there will never be another Fire Drake. He was the last of his kind, Mary. The last Fire Drake—*ever*. He died in part because you were too proud and stubborn to leave out a bowl of berries."

The queen of the Court of Light moved from Mary's ear to look her in the eye, gauging her reaction to the news of Awynn's passing. No sign of empathy or compassion graced the other monarch's face, not even for a moment. Mary only stared, her eyes vacant. The silence infuriated Aurora, evident from the abrupt appearance of a tornado whipping around Mary's room, throwing the lavish furniture about like trinkets from a dollhouse, splintering them into kindling as they struck the walls.

Aurora took a breath and gained her regal composure, but her eyes never left Mary, and they were resplendent in their green glow. She carefully chose her words. "Like father, like daughter. You are an insignificant worm. You humans are all the same—just a little power, and you believe you can rule the world. You think you are above it all. You can't rule without compassion, humility, and kindness—virtues you do not possess. Awynn died saving another Fae's life during an argument that your selfish act caused. I will not kill you, Mary, because your life shall be empty, much like your womb." Aurora let Mary soak the information in. Then she stopped hovering and paced the floor. "Here I find myself giving you the same warning I gave your father so many years ago. Do not go to my followers out of retaliation. If you do, I will see it as an act of war against the Fae. I will come for you, Mary. There will be nowhere for you to go and no one to protect you, least of all your God. He won't help you. My army is bigger, and you can't hide from the elements."

Mary mumbled, and Aurora leaned closer to hear her: "Turn, then, most gracious advocate, thine eyes of mercy toward us; and after this our exile show unto us the blessed fruit of thy womb."

Aurora's anger flared. "You dare pray! And ask *Him* for mercy? After I have said your insolence and ego have caused the death of my friend and bishop, a Fae who displayed nothing but compassion for every creature he met. Oh, Mary, you are a waste of a soul. A lost cause on whom the Creator will have no mercy. Please pray; fritter your breath away, for I happen to know a thing or two about your God. You cannot put yourself first, Him second, and commit horrible acts in His name. He tends to take issue with that."

Mary stopped praying.

"Oh, but before I go, dear Mary, I will make one amendment to my warning." Aurora gestured with her finger. "Your sister, Princess Elizabeth, will be the next queen of England. She is under Fae protection now—touch her, and I will come after you! I have a good feeling about her. She seems to possess qualities you lack, like a conscience." Aurora smirked. "I think when you pass on, which should be in about three years, judging by your light, the Fae will once again return to their alliance with the royal family."

The candles flickered out, and Mary's privy guard woke up. Seeing his queen on the floor, he ran over to her. Mary sat upright, trembling. Pale and clammy, her arms clasped her belly. Tears ran down her cheeks. She continued murmuring the same prayer line repeatedly: "Turn, then, most gracious advocate, thine eyes of mercy toward us; and after this our exile show unto us the blessed fruit of thy womb."

She did not speak for days to anyone, just repeated the line from the prayer. Periodically, she would check for bleeding, worrying about her baby. But after a month, Queen Mary recovered from what the doctors thought was exhaustion due to her pregnancy. She was assured the baby was fine and due in April.

Chapter Twenty-One:
A Promise Fulfilled
(April 30, 1555)

O n the morning of April 30, 1555, Queen Mary woke to her water breaking and labor pains. The birth chamber was readied, and Mary prepared for delivery. Meanwhile, the upstairs servants decorated the nursery with gifts from nobility, including a magnificently carved cradle from an unknown "friend." The cradle had what appeared to be dragons circling it while other dragons were depicted swallowing whole eggs from nests; inside the cradle were several swan feathers. The cradle was a portrait of war rather than a baby's lullaby, but the craftsmanship was breathtaking, overriding the scenery it portrayed.

For hours, Mary pushed, flanked by her midwives. When she thought she could not push anymore, she passed an unattached umbilical cord and placenta, indicating there once was a child. The midwives screamed. They held their queen on the birthing stool, as she was close to unconsciousness. Mary mumbled she wanted to see her baby, but there wasn't one. One brave midwife waded through the bloody remains and found a swan feather buried underneath the placenta, pure white, untouched by the blood and gore. She lifted it up and showed it to Queen Mary, who let out a bloodcurdling scream and collapsed.

Aurora was standing by her balcony when the wind carried Mary's scream to her. The Fae queen looked up and simply whispered, "For Awynn." She cradled the small creature stroking its back for a moment.

"Your Majesty?" a man's voice called from inside her private meeting chambers.

"Sir Arthur, thank you for coming."

"Of course. Bishop Ward said it was urgent."

Aurora strode over to the tall Fae. He had white hair much like Awynn, though it lacked his sparkle and the strands underneath were midnight black. She smiled, thinking of Awynn. "It is urgent but joyful as well." She opened her hands to present him with the newborn grey swan.

Sir Arthur looked from her to the swan several times. "Your Grace?"

"Sir Arthur, your line is no longer in danger of meeting their Oblivion. Welcome the product of your union with Queen Mary—it turns out the baby is more Fae than human." It wasn't necessary to tell him the ugly details of how this had come to be. Mary wasn't worthy of this precious gift.

Sir Arthur's eyes watered, and his smile grew bright. "He is Fae. He took on the shifting traits of my line. We have not seen a shifter in four hundred years."

Aurora watched, moved by how he cupped the creature, stroking the Little One's black bill and examining his webbed feet. He held the swan close to his heart, his pride and protectiveness evident.

"He is Fae and yours. Do you know when he will shift his form?" she inquired.

Sir Arthur continued to inspect every part of the small swan. "Usually in a few months, but since he was housed in a human womb, I'm not sure. To be honest, Your Majesty, I do not care. He is perfect; however long it takes, it does not matter. The Dinay Mera line is not lost. Thank you, Your Grace!" Sir Arthur bowed and exited, holding his newfound joy.

Aurora brought her hands to her lips, smiling.

Her mood was interrupted by long, drawn-out applause coming from the balcony. Queen Aurora was startled to see King Jarvok standing on her rose quartz veranda, uninvited.

Chapter Twenty-Two:
Being Pragmatic

Jarvok's usual midnight-black armor soaked in all the light; nothing reflected off of him. Instead, he stood drinking in the brightness. His normally imposing figure had taken on a casual demeanor, making him somehow even more intimidating. Aurora was used to seeing a viper coiled and ready to strike, not relaxing in the sun.

But Jarvok's penetrating amber glare conveyed pride. "I didn't think you had it in you, dear queen. Your sense of torture is almost worthy of a Dark Fae." Jarvok's husky voice was a lethal caress.

He uncrossed his hands from behind his back as he marched effortlessly toward her. For all of his size, Jarvok moved with liquid grace, each step a juxtaposition of thunder and lightning. The ground should have shaken from the size of him, yet he moved like fog rolling in.

Aurora did not flinch. She held his gaze and her ground, lifting her chin. "How did you get in here?"

Jarvok curled his lip. "Well, first of all, you did invite me months ago to witness my retribution, so here I am."

He held his hands away from his body as if presenting himself to her. "Second, we are outside, my dear. I can go anywhere I want. I do happen to know a flying dragon." Jarvok pointed to Dragor, who landed and perched himself on the railing of the veranda.

The dragon gave the queen a mocking head tilt as if conveying a sarcastic retort. Dragor snorted. Aurora imagined the dragon's response sounding something like "How do you think he got up here?"

Aurora raised her brow at the large, winged creature. "Dragor." She turned her full attention back to Jarvok. "What did you mean by having it in me? I told you I would handle things, and I did. Instead of standing here critiquing me, did you ever think what would happen if we united our courts, Jarvok, and actually helped each other?" Her hands circled before resting around her waist, a nervous tic, as the mocking remark left her lips.

Jarvok stood only a few feet away, pondering her question. His right index finger grazed his lips. For the first time since she could remember, he was not wearing full battle armor, only the Kyanite that was bonded to him. Aurora's eyes traced his luminescent skin. Slowly, she followed his Kyanite gauntlet from his right wrist, where the thick black crystalline edges seamlessly melded into the dermis. She couldn't tell where he began and the armor ended. Jarvok followed her gaze to his shoulder, where his pauldron melted into him.

Aurora broke the tension. "Well?" she said with an extra helping of sarcasm, hoping it would distract Jarvok from her staring.

Jarvok huffed and shook his head, breaking the thoughts of cooperation he may or may not have been considering. "So typical. You stare at me like I am a monster, but from what I gather, you emotionally tormented Queen Mary to exact your revenge, making her believe she gave birth to a feather. While in reality, you opened a portal at the moment of delivery and the Little One passed through the Veil. The queen has no idea the babe even exists. My dear Aurora, that is downright devious!" He covered his mouth, hiding his smirk.

Aurora tightened her mouth as her cheeks flushed. "Your point, Jarvok?"

"My scars are on the outside. I may not be appealing, but at least I call myself a Dark Fae, and the humans know what I am. We cut them, but they see it coming. You Light Fae make yourselves all pretty, but you are just as cold-blooded; the difference is you will cut them with a smile on your face, but because you use a clean blade, you think it hurts less. We are even. Your obligation is fulfilled. Go about your day, little queen. I am done with you." Jarvok's voice bordered on a growl. He waved dismissively and turned his back, walking toward Dragor.

Aurora shut her eyes in frustration. *How dare he pass judgment on me and the Court of Light! I fulfilled my end of the agreement, and now he comments on how I went about it? He was the one who acted like a petulant child a few months ago because his court had been dishonored. He acted like his feelings were the only ones that mattered.* Aurora was exhausted from bending to everyone's whim. Their cycles of emotions determined whether blood coated her hands or not. *I cannot live like this anymore.*

Aurora opened her eyes. Nearby, Jarvok mumbled trivializing quips as he readied Dragor. She sent a gust of wind toward him, and the large Dark Fae slightly skidded forward, the Kyanite of his boots digging into the quartz floor, scratching it.

Jarvok glanced over his shoulder. "Ohhhh. That tickled." A devilish grin spread across his face. Aurora's energy wings emerged. He licked his lips; he was itching for a fight with Aurora.

The two monarchs had never met in combat, although their armies had clashed many times over in the Great War. One of the many privileges of being a king or queen—there was always another willing to fight for you, and ultimately, lay down their life for your cause. Aurora had seen less battle than Jarvok. Desdemona protected her queen from the scars of warfare.

"Desdemona isn't here to shield you, little queen. Are you sure you want to dance?" His voice was smooth as velvet, non-threatening. His eyes gleamed.

Aurora gave him a bob of her head and hit him with another squall of wind. This one sent Jarvok sailing into the railing of the veranda, but he caught himself, pushing off the railing, and absorbing some of the shock as the rock crumbled.

She lifted her chin. "I don't need protection. I fight my own battles. Are *you* sure *you* want this dance?"

Jarvok shook the rubble off his hands and gave a low, guttural laugh. "Is that all you've got?"

A blue Kyanite staff extended from his left wrist, and he spun as he passed Aurora, circling the staff low to the floor, catching her ankles and sweeping her legs out from under her before she could react. She fell backward for a moment. Jarvok attempted to capitalize on her position, but the queen recovered and caught the air current. Hurled upright, she twisted in midair and then landed behind Jarvok, but not before she delivered a devastating sidekick to his lower right ribs. Jarvok caught his breath and smirked. He had underestimated her hand-to-hand combat skills. He wouldn't make the same mistake twice.

Aurora became overconfident after landing the one kick—*an amateur mistake*, Jarvok thought. She flew on a rush of air straight at Jarvok. He braced with a long front stance to meet the wind Aurora brought, and just before she barreled into him, Jarvok dropped to both knees and leaned backward. As Aurora flew over him, he reached up and grabbed her ankles, twisting the queen around and pulling her in. He elbowed her on the back of the head, stunning her. Then, he picked up her limp body and sent her hurtling over the railing to the ground below. Her gown billowed upward as the queen vanished, plummeting to her Oblivion.

Dragor galloped to his side in excitement, looking like an oversized black dog. The dragon and Dark Fae king looked pleased with themselves. "Well, my friend, our dear queen seems to have taken a bit of a tumble." The dragon huffed in agreement.

Jarvok simpered. "Let's go find Desdemona and see if she is in the mood for a tango." His grin turned into a mischievous sneer, but as the two walked away, mini cyclones dropped out of the perfectly blue sky. "Troll's balls!" Jarvok hissed, annoyed. "Of course, it could not be that easy."

Aurora materialized out of one of the many cyclones. Her gown was ripped, the sleeves hanging by their seams. Her hair whipped about in the wind as her shoulders rose up and down frenetically. Yet her eyes glowed brightly with power, bathing the entire veranda in green light. The determined queen said nothing; her unwavering glare conveyed absolute supremacy. She stood battle-ready, prepared to take on the king of the Dark Fae for the final time.

In one swift motion, Aurora twirled her arms above her head; her palms opened, and she pushed the air outward. All the cyclones combined. The Dark Fae king did not have enough time to run from the tornado. Aurora watched the king's jaw clench and his shoulders brace for the unavoidable collision. The king was swept up in a swirling mass of chaos. Aurora lifted her arms, using all the power she could muster, and commanded the cyclone into the atmosphere, where it carried Jarvok until the tempest disappeared.

The black dragon's purple-and-amber eyes grew wide as the scales tipped in the Light Fae queen's favor. Only a moment ago, her Oblivion seemed to be a foregone conclusion, and now, Jarvok had disappeared. Dragor gaped at Aurora and back to the sky. He looked torn on whether to attack her or go after his friend; he chose the latter. His black leather wings created a windstorm to rival Aurora's as his powerful back muscles contracted. His legs shook the crystal pillars. He jumped from the veranda, his wings expanding as he caught the air current, banked to the left, and propelled himself upward.

Once the large winged creature disappeared into the sky above, Aurora faltered, reaching for the quartz ledge, finally showing the battle had taken its toll on her. Wiping the sweat from her brow, she lifted her head to survey the clouds above her. She knew she did not have much time.

The dark clouds parted for the enormous dragon with each beat of his wings, disintegrating into the ether as he cut through them, driving him higher into the atmosphere. Dragor raced into the grey sky. The dark storm clouds twisted and swirled around him. There was no sign of the cyclone carrying Jarvok. The dragon searched anxiously for him. *How high did she throw him?* The dragon glided well above the clouds; he would not stop until he found his king. Jarvok had done the same for him once when Dragor had thought all hope was lost.

Dragor's father was Chief Peandro of the Fire-Breathers and leader of the Draconians. Dragor would have assumed his father's role, but he did not light the Sacred Fire when he came of age. His father labeled him a disgrace and, by Draconian law, ordered him sacrificed to the Spark of Life's Fire god in the Sacred Mountain or else risk a curse on the Draconians. His father's proclamation of death still echoed in Dragor's head. Jarvok had interceded on behalf of Dragor and all Draconians who were to be sacrificed, challenging Chief Peandro to a fight to the death in the Draconian tradition—the three rings of fire, ice, and acid—for Dragor's freedom. Jarvok had won, choosing to take Dragor as his, treating him like a son, giving him the respect and love Peandro never had. Years later, Jarvok had returned Dragor to the Impolita Valley, the site of the Sacred Fire, and asked him to try to light it again. This time the dragon succeeded, giving Dragor the right to become chief of the Draconian Faction.

Dragor would not disappoint Jarvok. The dragon shook his head and let out a roar, his plating compressing around his jaw. There was a click of his back teeth, and the clouds were illuminated with his purple fire. In the distance, a figure was suspended in a swirling cloud. *Jarvok!* The cloud of spiraling wind slowly dissipated. The fierce dragon used all his strength to soar as fast as he could to the king before the cloud dropped him. As the last swirl rotated, releasing Jarvok's limp body, Dragor swooped in and caught his longtime companion. The dragon exhaled, relief washing over him. Jarvok stirred, and Dragor glanced back, knowing revenge would be Jarvok's best medicine.

Aurora gathered her fortitude. She wanted to believe she had defeated Jarvok, but she knew never to underestimate the Dark Fae king. As if on cue, an ominous shadow eclipsed the sun above her. Dragor landed on her veranda, and he wasn't happy, his sickle tail snapping. Aurora backed up from the brutal winged beast, his hot breath burning her skin. With each placement of his claws, the veranda shook, but she held her ground. Aurora would not show fear to this creature anymore.

With a loud whistle, Desdemona appeared, vaulting off the top of the nearby tower and landing in between the queen and the dragon, her Harbinger swords drawn.

"Stay where you are, beast!" she commanded. Dragor looked indignant. He drew in a breath, an audible click coming from the rear of his mouth as his back teeth struck together like flint and tinder. His purple feathers waved as the plating compressed. However, before he could exhale, Jarvok spoke, his voice hoarse as he raised his hand to his throat.

"Enough, Dragor." It was a request, not a command. Jarvok respected Dragor too much to belittle the dragon in front of the Light Fae.

Dragor turned his long neck in a fluid, undulating motion and shot his fire at a nearby stone statue, melting it. His scaled neck plates compressed, pushing out the contents of the gas bladders before returning to their fanned-out position, reloaded and ready to strike should Dragor decide to use his oral defense again. The dragon glanced back at Aurora and Desdemona—a clear warning Jarvok had just saved them from a charbroiling. The Dark Fae king slid off Dragor and stepped forward, but Desdemona kept her guard up—swords crossed in front of her chest, feet planted.

"I'm tiring of these games, Aurora. Let's end this." He raised his arms, and Dragor stepped up behind him.

ART BY RUXANDRA TUDORICĂ ◦ AMETHYSS DIGITAL ARTIST

It seems our two monarchs are headed for one last show-down, and Jarvok has a trick up his Kyanite gauntlet. Place your bets, my Fae friends! Queen Aurora, King Jarvok, and all the Fae will return, very soon in *Birth of the Fae: From the Ashes*. Until then, please keep up on all things Fae on Instagram: @BirthoftheFae_novel and at www.Birthofthefae.com

CHAOS BE WITH YOU!

~Danielle

4 Horsemen Publications

Romance

Ann Shepphird
The War Council

Emily Bunney
All or Nothing
All the Way
All Night Long: Novella
All She Needs
Having it All
All at Once
All Together
All for Her

Lynn Chantale
The Baker's Touch
Blind Secrets
Broken Lens

Mimi Francis
Private Lives
Private Protection
Run Away Home
The Professor

Fantasy, SciFi, & Paranormal Romance

Beau Lake
The Beast Beside Me
The Beast Within Me
Taming the Beast: Novella
The Beast After Me
Charming the Beast: Novella
The Beast Like Me
An Eye for Emeralds
Swimming in Sapphires
Pining for Pearls

D. Lambert
To Walk into the Sands
Rydan
Celebrant
Northlander
Esparan

King
Traitor
His Last Name

J.M. Paquette
Klauden's Ring
Solyn's Body
The Inbetween
Hannah's Heart
Call Me Forth
Invite Me In
Keep Me Close

Lyra R. Saenz
Prelude
Falsetto in the Woods: Novella

Ragtime Swing
Sonata
Song of the Sea
The Devil's Trill
Bercuese
To Heal a Songbird
Ghost March
Nocturne

Sessrúmnir

VALERIE WILLIS
Cedric: The Demonic Knight
Romasanta: Father of
Werewolves
The Oracle: Keeper of the
Gaea's Gate
Artemis: Eye of Gaea
King Incubus: A New Reign

T.S. SIMONS
Antipodes
The Liminal Space
Ouroboros
Caim

V.C. WILLIS
Prince's Priest
Priest's Assassin

YOUNG ADULT FANTASY

BLAISE RAMSAY
Through The Black Mirror
The City of Nightmares
The Astral Tower
The Lost Book of the Old Blood
Shadow of the Dark Witch
Chamber of the Dead God

Broken Beginnings:
Story of Thane
Shattered Start: Story of Sera
Sins of The Father:
Story of Silas
Honorable Darkness: Story of
Hex and Snip
A Love Lost: Story of Radnar

C.R. RICE
Denial
Anger
Bargaining
Depression
Acceptance

VALERIE WILLIS
Rebirth
Judgment
Death

4HORSEMENPUBLICATIONS.COM

9 781644 504079